The Devil's Claim

Maria Kovac

Copywright © 2024 Maria Kovac

All rights reserved

No part of this publication may be distributed, reproduced or transmitted in any form or by any means, including photocopying, recording or other electronic or mechanical methods, without the prior permission of the author.

Edited by Stephen Black.

Cover art by Grim Poppy Design.

"The greatest trick the Devil pulled was convincing the world there was only one of him."

David Wong

PROLOGUE

Grožnjan, Croatia 1978

The room was silent, except for the hum of the ceiling fan overhead. Beads of sweat trickled down the forehead of the young priest as he sat on the edge of the bed, where the body of the girl lay. His breath came in heavy rasps as he gripped the bed frame beneath, fighting back the tears.

He had failed her.

Earlier that day, when the girl's mother had phoned the rectory, he had heard a cacophony of noise in the background as she'd pleaded for someone to come.

"Quickly, please! My daughter, she needs help – it's going to kill her!"

"Slow down please," he had said calmly. "What has happened? What exactly is going to kill your daughter?"

In the midst of her frantic cries, there was no mistaking the roaring voice which erupted in the room behind her.

It was a noise only the Devil himself could make. Upon hearing the sound, he felt an excruciating pain pass through his head, making him cry out. He recognised it immediately as a psychic attack, a phenomenon experienced most commonly amongst clairvoyants when encountering a spirit. However, it was also shared by those in the priesthood when attacked by malevolent, demonic forces. Slamming down the receiver, he had poured himself a shot of whiskey with trembling hands before hastily making his way to the home of the young girl. He knew what he had to do, and there was very little time to get it done.

On arrival at the Pavic residence, he was greeted by the distraught mother, who ushered him inside and up to the bedroom of her teenage daughter, Elena. Reluctant to enter, the mother stayed at the threshold, fearful at what lay within. The priest entered without her and closed the door behind him.

What first struck him, upon entering the room, was the overpowering stench. It smelled of death and decay. Ahead of him, he could see the writhing, tethered body of Elena squirming on soiled bedsheets, resembling a living corpse. Sunken black eyes, sallow skin, and a crater of a mouth that looked as if it had collapsed in on itself.

At the sight of him standing in the doorway, Elena had stopped her writhing and turned her head in his direction, her hard stare burning into him. Her face had cracked into an ugly sneer, and when she had opened her mouth to speak, the priest could see she was missing all of her teeth.

"Hello, priest" growled a deep, mocking voice from Elena's blackened lips, her head cocked in curiosity as her dark eyes met his. The sinister tone of her voice left the young priest feeling cold, despite the forty-degree heat outside.

"You are a long way from home," it hissed.

"What do you want with the girl?" the priest asked boldly, trying not to show any semblance of fear.

The entity in front of him grinned. He knew he was not speaking with Elena.

"She is but a vessel," it said, peering ever more closely at him. "But it would appear I've seen something I like the look of more. Why don't you come closer, priest? I can smell something in your fear. Is it guilt, perhaps? Let me taste your sin." It sneered as a blackened tongue rolled over parched, sunken lips.

A rage clouded over the young priest as he rushed towards the girl. All fear of the entity possessing her had evaporated at the threat of exposing the weight of the sin he carried heavily within him; a sin so great he beat himself each day until he bled. Raw memories of the young girl back home in Donegal flooded his mind and he saw red. She had told him she was seventeen; he hadn't meant to get her pregnant, and when he pushed her down the stairs had never meant to kill her, only the new life growing inside of her. In his panic, he had disposed of her body in the river. When it had been retrieved some weeks later, all fingers pointed to the stepfather, which the young priest had been grateful for; he knew then he would be indebted to God for the rest of his days for his crime going unpunished. That was when he had decided to take the cloth and show penance each day for the guilt and shame he silently endured. He hoped giving his life over to God would absolve him of his sins.

As he lunged at Elena's throat, he momentarily glimpsed the fear in her eyes as she battled against the entity within, but it was too late. Releasing his grip, she fell into cardiac arrest, and, as he cradled the dying girl in his arms and watched the life drain from her eyes, he saw a glimmer of the demon inside her again as it grinned up at him.

"We'll meet again, priest."

1

London 2023

Strange activity had begun soon after moving into the new house. The move was intended to repair their marriage, but it had been as effective as an ill-fitting plaster placed over a gaping wound. No matter how hard Anna had tried to hold it together, it just would not heal. The rot in their marriage had become gangrenous.

Anna and James Hayward had bought the house through auction, a move offering the prospect of a fresh start together, somewhere new. It was a spacious Victorian townhouse situated in the leafy and prestigious Belsize Park. The house was at the top end of a smart tree lined street leading down to Primrose Hill, set back from the road, with a red and black checkerboard pathway leading up to an imposing black front door. Sprawling purple wisteria scaled the white exterior of the house, which brought a softness to the grandeur of the property. Anna had fallen in love with it before she had even set foot inside. She had felt the house calling to her. Once the couple stepped inside, they fell under the spell of its charm and knew it was the house for them. They were giddy with excitement at the prospect of having the opportunity to own such a magnificent house, and Anna hoped it would be the place where they would eventually raise a family. It was only later they discovered it was under tragic circumstances that the house had come to auction. Upon purchase, they were informed that the previous owner had vacated the property after his wife had unexpectedly died, the circumstances of which were undisclosed. Despite this, Anna and James were determined not to let this overshadow what would be a beautiful home for them.

James' job regularly took him away from London, which put a strain on the relationship after his affair, from which Anna was still reeling but trying her best to move on from.

She had come home from work early one day and had been surprised to see his car on the drive. On entering the house, she had heard muffled voices coming from upstairs and a woman laughing. Feeling sick to the stomach, as she crept upstairs, Anna was fearful of what she would walk in on. The bedroom door was ajar, and she had caught sight of a young, blonde woman in bed with her husband. The room smelled heavily of sex and weed. Neither had noticed Anna, as she stood watching from the crack in the doorway. Her breath caught in her throat as she was rooted to the spot, not knowing what to do. Part of her wanted to burst in and claw the faces off both of them, while the other wanted to flee, pretending she hadn't seen a thing, and this had all been a bad dream. She had watched, as her husband had thrown the woman onto her back and buried his head between her legs - something he'd always told Anna he hated doing. Her body had writhed under James' touch, shaking as he brought her to orgasm, making Anna's stomach churn in horror.

Unable to believe her eyes, and in denial of what she had witnessed, Anna had backed away from the bedroom and the sound of the woman's climactic cries. Her eyes had stung as she held back the tears and crept back downstairs, closing the front door quietly behind her, with trembling hands.

She had sat for a few moments in her car opposite the house and wept, allowing the tears to flow freely before starting the engine. Circling the neighbourhood several times, Anna had gripped the steering wheel tightly until her knuckles had turned white, finally allowing the rage to boil over. Only then could she emit the loud roar that she had been holding in since leaving the house. She had driven aimlessly, eyes burning from the tears as she had considered her options. She had told herself that, if she confronted James, he would leave her, and she was too scared to be alone. She would rather share him than lose him altogether, especially to another woman. Years of narcissistic abuse had left her a shell of the woman she had used to be, and she feared no other man would want her as she couldn't believe she was deserving of love.

    She had told herself this must all be her fault, as she obviously wasn't giving her husband what he needed. She made a pledge that she would start making more effort with herself and find ways to keep things exciting; then he would have no reason to stray. Intrusive thoughts continued to flood her mind as she drove. She wondered if perhaps it was the fact she had put on weight in recent months or maybe she wasn't making enough effort to keep James happy in bed; they rarely had sex anymore, as he worked so late and complained of being tired all the time. It hadn't occurred to her that he might have been having sex with someone else.

Her mind scoured the possibilities of why it must be her fault, but she still convinced herself she could fix their marriage.

Driving past Highgate Cemetery, Anna felt an overpowering urge to pull over. It was starting to rain, and the tumultuous sky cast an eerie blue glow over the cemetery. She walked through the unlocked iron gates and ventured inside. Wandering along the sinuous pathways and past ivy-clad monuments, she emerged from the gloomy Egyptian Avenue into the Circle of Lebanon. Here lay an open circle of mausoleums and tombs, named after the remains of an ancient Cedar of Lebanon tree that the vaults were built around. The tree was long gone, but the area had retained its name.

As Anna sat, and took stock of her surroundings, a dark thought crept into her head. She had heard about people selling their soul to the Devil in exchange for something they wanted in return. She didn't want to go so far as to sell her soul, but she wondered if a deal could be struck in another way. Perhaps if she opened herself up, she could attract help from a powerful entity, one that could empower her to be desired once more.

She closed her eyes, imagining her body being used in a way that made her feel wanted. *Desired.* She smiled, as she pictured strong hands resting on her throat and pushing her down onto her bed. The full weight of an unseen force pressing against her, taking ownership as she gave herself over unconditionally to it.

As her imagination soared at the thought of her body being craved and used by such an enigma, she could feel her grief lift and turn instead to anger. She wanted to teach James and his lover a lesson. As a young child, her Hungarian grandmother had taught her much of the old Romani ways. A hex or curse could be placed on someone, but they had to be used with caution, as it wasn't just the words that carried the power but the intention as well; and once the intention had been cast, it wasn't always easy to lift. She had once heard her grandmother utter words to warn someone's wish from becoming their worst nightmare. She had never once considered that she would use those very same words about her own husband.

"A legnagyobb kívánságod lesz a legrosszabb rémálmod," she mouthed under her breath, uttering each word with intent. No sooner had the words left her mouth, she could feel the energy around her change.

She opened her eyes with a start as a sudden chill passed through her, feeling something brush her shoulder.

Turning around, she was sure she saw the shadow of something move between the vaults.

"Hello? Is anyone there?" she called out shakily, suddenly aware of how vulnerable she was, sat alone in the cemetery.

Her voice echoed around the circle of tombs, and she thought she heard the crunch of leaves behind one, as if someone had stepped on them.

Overcome with fear, she clutched her coat tightly around her and hurried away from the winding mausoleums, making her way towards the exit. It was almost dark, and they'd be locking the gates soon, although she had thought it strange that she hadn't seen another soul since entering the cemetery.

Casting a glance back at the cemetery, as she sped off in her car, she couldn't shake off the sensation that she was being followed. She had sensed eyes on her since leaving the Circle, so now placed her foot on the accelerator. As she made her way home, she felt the fog lift and knew what she needed to do in order to make her husband desire her again.

This other woman wasn't going to be a problem for much longer.

Anna was never one for being impulsive. However, she decided to stop off at a nearby pharmacy and bought a tube of bold red lipstick. She rarely wore makeup and had never worn red lipstick before. James had once told her he thought it slutty, and that she shouldn't be drawing attention to herself like that. Her brow furrowed in rage as she remembered how he had made her feel.

Pulling up outside, she stared at the house from the confines of her car. The kitchen light was on, and she could see James sitting at the table. He was looking down at his phone, smiling. Anna felt a pang of anger but swallowed it down. She ran a brush through her hair and pulled the lipstick from her bag, applying it generously. She pursed her lips as she admired her reflection. She looked different. Perhaps it was the lipstick, but her eyes looked bluer and had a certain sparkle to them, which she hadn't noticed before. For the first time in so long, she felt attractive.

That's more like it, she thought to herself in a voice that sounded different to her own.

Slamming the car door shut behind her, she strode purposefully up to the house. In the time between discovering her husband's infidelity and returning home, she now knew it was time to leave meek, submissive Anna behind, in exchange for a bold, confident Anna worthy of love and respect. It was her man sitting in that house, and nobody was going to get in the way of that.

2

The house move happened suddenly. Anna had decided a fresh start would do them both good and that having something new to get excited about just might bring the spark back to their stagnant marriage. In the days following her discovery of James' philandering, the new house had jumped out at Anna from the pages of the auction listing. She felt drawn to it before even visiting and, to her surprise, the possibility also excited James, who was still none the wiser that she knew about his infidelity.

For a while after the move, their marriage had felt revived. Anna enjoyed having James around more, spending their weekends together decorating and choosing things to furnish their new home. He even hinted at turning the smallest bedroom into a nursery, which surprised Anna as he had always been opposed to the idea of having children. Spending more time together had brought them closer, and the sex was incredible. As her appetite for sex increased, so did his.

She had noticed James paying her more attention than usual. She would go to the gym most days, and her body was starting to show positive changes, which came from all the hours she was putting in. She had coloured her mousy hair a striking shade of auburn, making her blue eyes come alive. She had also started to initiate sex regularly and would enjoy showing off her body to him, wearing beautiful lingerie.

She had surprised him one evening, as he walked in the door, by taking his coat from him. Without saying a word, she had slipped out of her robe, wearing nothing but white lace panties, before getting down on her knees. She looked up at him doe eyed as she undid his belt, pulling his jeans down and taking the full length of his cock in her willing mouth. She thought she could taste another woman on him, yet she pushed that thought out of her head as she sucked him hungrily.

James was taken aback with her forwardness, as he had never seen this side of Anna throughout their marriage, where before sex had always felt laborious. Sweet, submissive Anna who did as she was told, but their vanilla sex life had been virtually non-existent. Yet now, as he looked down at her bobbing head and ran his hands through her flaming red locks, watching as she eagerly took his hot seed in her mouth, he couldn't help but feel a pang of lust for her. He was incapable of feeling love, but lust was something he had plenty of to share.

He pulled her up by the hair to face him, brushing his hand across her throat, before tossing her over onto her front, so that she was leaning across the bureau in the hallway facing the mirror. Pushing his hand on her back to keep her in place, he thrust himself into her from behind with force, hearing her gasp as he filled her with his erect length. Anna had never let James fuck her like this before, but something had awoken inside her, casting aside all inhibitions. She wanted to be fucked hard. Devoured. She lifted her head, watching him from the mirror, as he continued to frantically pound in and out of her, her eyes never leaving his as they eventually came together in explosive passion.

This newfound limerence, however, was to be short-lived. Within a few months of moving into the house, James began sliding into old habits, working late again as the business trips became more frequent. Anna was soon beginning to spend more time alone, and the shine of the new house began to wear thin. She started to look at it differently. She noticed how tired it looked, despite the fresh paint, which seemed to peel within weeks of the walls being coated, and how cold it always felt, even in the height of summer. It was an old house, so the cracks in the walls hadn't bothered them at first, opting to cover them with framed pictures which hid them for a while; however, within a matter of months the cracks had crept beyond the frames.

The problems seemed to worsen when Anna was alone in the house. She began to get worried and doubt herself, knowing she had locked the front door each night only to come downstairs in the morning to find it unlocked. A growing sense of oppressiveness permeated the place, and she found herself wanting to spend more time out of it when James was away. She found it difficult to settle and doubts were creeping into her head as to whether buying the house had been a mistake. The neighbours were unfriendly as well, and upon seeing Anna would pretend not to notice her and scuttle back inside, or distract themselves with something to avoid eye contact or conversation.

It was also around this time that Anna started to notice sudden movements out of the corner of her eye. Little things at first that she put down to tricks of the light. These occurrences would usually happen at night and always when she was alone. There were times when she switched the television off and, for a moment, she thought she caught sight in the reflection of a dark figure standing in the doorway; yet when she turned around there would be nothing there. Often, she would come home and find the television or radio on, when she knew she had switched everything off. Occasionally, she would wake in the early hours of the morning to the sound of the television playing downstairs. She would tell herself it was an old house, so it was most likely an electrical glitch, as the alternative seemed too uncomfortable to consider.

She also started to have unsettling dreams. Memories of the car accident which had killed her parents resurfaced to haunt her. In the dreams, she would see her dead mother standing in front of her at the foot of the bed, bloodied and missing an eye from where she had been thrown through the windscreen and impaled on a rod of steel. Her father had been decapitated when the car had overturned. The recurring nightmare would have her mother cradling her father's severed head before extending her arms to offer it to Anna. As she opened her mouth to speak, maggots and dirt would fall from it. In each dream her mother would be standing a little closer than the time before, her body in a more advanced state of decomposition. A stench of decay would accompany her which, upon waking, would fill Anna's nostrils as she lay terrified in soaked sheets, afraid to shut her eyes again for fear of what she might dream of next.

As time went on, Anna became more sleep deprived and began to sense an energy around her. The energy felt dark, to the point where it was almost suffocating. The feeling reminded her of what she had experienced at Highgate Cemetery all those months ago. She initially put it down to her brain playing tricks on her from the lack of sleep, but the niggle in the back of the mind couldn't erase it completely. It was the same energy she had felt when she had the compulsion to buy the red lipstick, then hair dye, and, most recently, a pack of cigarettes. She hadn't smoked in years because James loathed it, but shortly after discovering his affair, the voice in her head, which had taken on the same unfamiliar tone as before, had persuaded her to do it.

Why not? Fuck what he thinks, you can do as you please.

With James' absences becoming ever more frequent, Anna's need for sexual gratification intensified. She found herself trawling the city bars, sitting alone and dressed provocatively to pick up men or women for sex. She would play the part of a woman travelling alone on business looking for hook-ups with no strings attached, and whether it was the allure of her pheromones or her newly found seductive charm, she discovered that she could make almost any person she wanted fall at her feet. She had never so much as kissed a woman before, but this newfound sexual appetite had her craving the touch and taste of them just as much as any man.

    The first woman she had brought home for sex had been called Zoe, whom she had particularly liked and learned a lot from. She was a few years older than Anna and was well-versed in what women liked. Zoe had been sitting with friends at a goth bar in Camden, when Anna had walked in and caught her eye as she passed. Moments later, she slipped in next to her at the bar and the pair had got talking. With black, Bettie Paige style bangs, plump red lips and caramel skin adorned with tattoos, Anna had felt the excitement inside her stir. Many shots later, after a drunken fumble in the pub toilets, Zoe had accompanied her home.

    Grabbing a bottle of wine from the fridge and two glasses, Anna had led her upstairs to the bedroom. Zoe had taken the wine from Anna's hand, placing it on the bedside table before smiling and pushing her back onto the bed. Anna had raised herself up to watch as Zoe had kneeled in front of her, sliding her hands up Anna's dress to remove her knickers, which were already soaked in anticipation.

Locking eyes with Anna, she had run her tongue over her before burying her head between Anna's thighs, exploring her wet folds with her dextrous tongue until she came in sustained waves.

The sex was different to how she had experienced it with men. Zoe knew just what to do to get her off and to keep her coming multiple times. It had awakened a suppressed desire within her, one that she hadn't explored before. Anna's rule up until meeting her had been to never sleep with the same person again; the sex was just a hook-up. No numbers would be exchanged, and they would never stay the night. However, there was something about Zoe that she liked, and they met up a handful of times before Zoe's number went dead and she never heard from her again. Anna visited the bar where they had met several times after that, hoping to bump into her, but she never appeared.

It was shortly after Zoe's disappearance that she met him. He was different from the rest. She had already discovered she could smell the sexual desire of others from a distance and knew who to make a play for, but this one she couldn't read. She had spotted him, sitting alone in a cocktail lounge, studying her from across the room as he took long drags from a cigarette. She placed him at around fifty, well dressed in an expensive looking black, tailored suit. His raven hair, scattered with grey flecks, framed a weathered, yet handsome, face. Dark eyes, and a five o'clock shadow, framed a strong jawline with soft, inviting lips. She could feel the weight of his stare from across the room, and each time she met his eye, she felt compelled to look away. His energy was intimidating yet intoxicating.

As she sat sipping her martini, she could feel his eyes undressing her, feasting on her body, and her pulse quickened as he rested his gaze between her legs. She was aware of how good she looked that night, her fiery locks cascading over her shoulders in loose waves, almost skimming her waist as it had grown so exponentially over the last few months. A black cocktail dress amplified her curves, exposing a hint of cleavage as it clung tightly to her slender waist. The smoky liner served to accentuate her blue eyes, and her red painted lips with defined cupid's bow, looked plumper than usual. She skimmed the rim of her glass with the scarlet painted talons of one hand as she circled the outline of her lips with the other in a tantalising way, lifting her head to meet his hard stare. She bit her lip and reached for her cigarettes, locking eyes with him as she lit one, inhaling the smoke deeply.

He smiled. It was a dry smile, and, in the dim light, it almost looked mocking, but she couldn't be sure. She licked her lips and finished her drink. The man raised his glass and pointed to it, gesturing whether she would like another. Anna nodded before hearing the voice in her head again.

Dry martini?

Yes.

The man summoned over the waiter, never once breaking eye contact with Anna.

Come here.

Anna found herself walking over towards the man. She felt naked as his eyes continued to undress her, and she could feel herself tingling with lust.

"How did you do that?" she asked as she approached the table.

"Do what?" he replied.

"You know exactly what I mean. It was like you could read my mind."

The man smiled. This time Anna was sure it was mocking. "I don't know what you mean. But since you are here, care to join me?"

The waiter returned, carrying a tray with two martinis, and Anna's heart thudded as she realised, he had been communicating telepathically with her from across the room.

"Who are you?" she asked nervously.

"Does it matter? I don't think you came over here to ask me my name," the man replied. His voice was soft, yet commanding, with a hint of an accent that Anna couldn't quite place. Eastern European, perhaps, but she couldn't be sure. He toyed with the zipper lighter between his fingers in such a dextrous manner, she wondered what else he could do with his hands.

"I came over to ask how you were able to tap into my head like that," she said.

"I don't know what you are talking about," he answered wryly, expelling a line of smoke in her direction. "My guess is you heard what you wanted to hear. Now why don't you tell me what really made you come over?"

"But the drink, how did you know?"

"It's not hard to tell from the glass what you were drinking. A reputable establishment such as this wouldn't consider serving martini in anything else," he smirked, nodding to her drink.

Anna flushed and bit her lip, accepting the man's valid explanation, and slid down to take her seat opposite him. Up close, his eyes looked even darker, black almost. They danced as he spoke to her, like dark pools of obsidian. His gaze was magnetic, and she felt compelled to return it.

She could feel the sexual tension between them simmer as she took a sip of her drink.

"My name's Anna," she said, smiling at her mystery companion.

"Samael," he answered.

"Is that a take on Samuel?"

"Not exactly." His face momentarily darkened at her question. "I go by many names, but not that."

"Where are you from?" she asked.

"Here and there. I've made my home here for some time now. London has all the carnal pleasures one could wish for, wouldn't you agree, Anna?"

Anna could feel her face flush once more. She could not understand how this man was getting under her skin in such a way. She had found herself the one who had been in control with the many lovers she had met over recent months, yet sitting opposite Samael she felt exposed and vulnerable.

He studied her intently from across the table, reaching for her hand and tracing his fingers across her palm. "You seem like a worldly woman, Anna. There is no need to be shy with me. I think we can both benefit from what the other has to offer."

As Anna looked up to meet his gaze again, she found herself nodding in agreement. She felt her pulse quicken as she imagined this man dominating her. Worshipping her body like the goddess she was.

The rest of the evening went by in a blur. Samael was the charming gentleman, every so often brushing his hand over hers as he spoke, leaving goosebumps on Anna's skin with every touch. As she sipped her third drink, she could feel the effects of the herbaceous liquor going to her head.

"It's probably time I thought about heading home," she said.

"Oh, that's a pity, we were only just getting started, and I was enjoying getting to know you."

Samael placed a hand gently on her chin to steer her gaze back to his. There was something about his eyes, familiar yet unsettling. Whenever they locked on hers, she felt her inhibitions lower as if she were under his spell.

"Well, I don't live far from here so why don't you come back to mine, and we can have another drink there?"

The man gently swept Anna's hair behind her shoulder as he leaned across the table.

"That sounds wonderful," he whispered as his lips grazed her ears, making her skin tingle in delight.

They couldn't keep their hands off each other in the cab back to the house. By the time they had reached the front door, Anna had removed his tie and started to unbutton his shirt. As they slammed the door behind them, he pushed her up against the wall and tugged at her dress, exposing her aroused nipples, which he locked his lips around, biting gently. Anna moaned, as one hand gripped her throat, squeezing it softly, while the other reached between her legs. His fingers found their way inside her wet sex, and she gasped as they arched in search of her sweet spot.

She glanced over his shoulder into the mirror, watching him fuck her like a hungry wolf. A large serpent tattoo coiled across his back, which struck her as strange as it was remarkably similar to one that Zoe had, and in the dim light of the hallway it looked to be moving. Thoughts of Zoe left her mind quickly, however, as she felt an overwhelming urge to taste him, licking his neck before skimming it with her teeth. Her appetite for him was insatiable.

"Upstairs," she pleaded.

She pulled him by the hand upstairs towards the bedroom, leaving their clothes strewn across the hallway floor. As they entered the bedroom, he threw her onto the bed and knelt in front of her, spreading her legs. His eyes looked like they were glowing as he held her gaze, edging his face closer between her thighs. She groaned as his tongue swept over her wet folds, circling her clit with intent, before beginning to work her harder with his fingers.

"Fuck me," she begged. "Please…I need you inside me."

He climbed up towards her, and she gasped as his cock brushed against the inside of her thigh.

"You want me inside you? Are you sure?" he growled in her ear.

"Yes," she moaned. "I need you."

He thrust himself inside her, and Anna was consumed with a mixture of pain and pleasure as her soft folds enveloped his full length. He threw her legs over his shoulders as he thrust deeper, making Anna cry out in ecstasy with every quickening stroke.

She had never had sex like it, not even with Zoe. Until now, she had thought what she had with James, and the random strangers she met in bars, could satisfy her, but on meeting this man, she realised what she had been craving all along and only he could give it to her.

She woke the next morning with a thumping headache. She opened her eyes and, for a moment, had forgotten about the events of the previous night but was promptly reminded, when she looked down at herself naked under the sheets, a throbbing tenderness between her legs.

She rolled over, half hoping to see Samael laying asleep next to her, despite her rule, but the bed was empty.

She got up and threw on a robe before making her way downstairs. There was no sign of him anywhere, so she figured he must have left hours ago. She paused when she walked past the front door, as the chain was on.

How is that possible? He must have let himself out through the back door, but why?

Anna walked through the kitchen to the back door. That was locked too. She was starting to feel uneasy. How could someone leave the house but secure it from the inside? If her body hadn't been throbbing in the way it was, then she could have sworn she had imagined the whole thing.

I must have let him out, when I was still drunk or half asleep, and I just can't remember.

Shrugging it off to a hazy head, she went back upstairs to shower away the events of the night before. Somehow though, she had a feeling it wouldn't be the last she would see of the strange, but irresistible, Samael.

3

It was shortly after the evening Anna brought Samael home that the scratching started.

At around three each night, without fail, she would wake to the same, eerie sound.

Scratch...

The noise would permeate from the walls around her, but Anna couldn't pinpoint the exact location. It sounded like it was coming from inside the room, like long fingernails being dragged slowly down a blackboard, intensifying each time, until it stopped abruptly. The scratching was also accompanied by a pungent smell. The odour reminded Anna of a dead rat she had found in the attic once. It seemed to seep throughout the house, filling her nostrils to the point she couldn't escape it, even upon leaving. It had reached the stage where she was concerned the smell might even be coming from her.

James was away on a lengthy business trip to Hong Kong and was, for the most part, unobtainable. After a week of the scratching and strange odour, Anna called in pest control, as it seemed mice were the only feasible explanation. She explained how she had been hearing strange noises at night, and the man from the agency agreed it was most likely rodents. He set traps with poison around the house, yet seemed surprised there was no visible sign of anything present and was unable to detect a smell in the property. There was a possibility, he told her, that the mice could be living inside the walls, which could explain the noises. A dead one would also explain the smell she had experienced.

Over the coming weeks, the noises continued to worsen and sounded like they were getting closer. The smell had also become sicklier, resembling something badly infected, like an oozing wound that had become gangrenous. Despite this, the traps remained intact and the poison untouched, so Anna tried to bury the thought to the back of her mind.

Something must be rotting in the walls. Either that or I'm going mad…

But soon, these oddities were accompanied by another disturbance. Anna began to experience severe episodes of sleep paralysis.

This wasn't just the usual case of her body being in sleep mode while her brain was active. The dread which accompanied it shook Anna to the very core. Each night, in a dreamlike state, she would be aware of a crushing heaviness on her chest, accompanied by a consuming sense of terror and an inability to move a muscle. It felt like the bed covers were smothering her, and her arms and legs were like dead weights. These episodes would continue nightly, all while James was away, and she would be rooted to the spot, aware of a black mass present in the room with her. The mass originated at the foot of the bed, drawing closer each time, until it was crouched over her chest, so close she could have touched it, had she been able to move.

It came to a head one night in November, when Anna was alone in the house as James was away on yet another trip. She woke as usual at three, pinned to the bed and unable to move; but this time an eruption of whispers filled the room. She could make out what sounded to be three or four different voices but was unable to make any sense of what was being said. The babbling sounded like an ancient tongue, and the voices seemed to resonate from every corner of the room. Then she heard a male voice summoning her over the cacophony of disembodied voices.

Anna.

There was no mistaking the sound of her name being called. Unable to shake free from the paralysis, she panicked and squeezed her eyes tightly shut, too scared to open them for fear of what, or whom, she might see.

Give yourself to me, Anna...

Don't deny me.

The voice felt closer, and her ear filled with warm, heavy breathing. Slowly, the bedsheets inched down, exposing her nakedness, but rather than feeling compelled to cover herself, Anna was rooted to the spot and allowed the covers to continue to slide. Whatever was in the room seemed to have control over her, as she couldn't budge an inch, nor did she want to. She could feel a heaviness settle over her chest, yet still refrained from opening her eyes. Terror may have paralysed her body, but her mind craved what was coming next. Conversely, she felt herself beginning to get aroused as invisible hands placed themselves on her throat, squeezing gently before moving down over her breasts to between her legs, firmly pushing them apart. She could feel a gush of wetness as the unseen force pressed itself against her. She gasped as she sensed a warm tongue slowly circle her clit and then centre itself on the spot James could never reach. Only one man had ever worked his tongue like that on her before.

No, it couldn't be.

One hand made its way back to her throat before brushing against her nipples, making them hard and aching to be sucked and squeezed. The heavy force pushed her down deeper into the mattress as she felt her legs being spread further apart, and she cried out in pleasure as she felt the sheer force of the entity pushing its way inside her. It thrust into her aggressively, but Anna didn't fight it. Instead, she gave herself over to it, allowing its unnatural length and girth to consume her until she came in thundering waves.

It was then that she felt the entity retract and the heaviness in the room lift. She was alone again. Anna fell into a deep, satisfied, trance-like sleep and, upon waking, wasn't sure if she had imagined the events of the previous night. She glanced over to the clock and saw it read 08.37.

Fuck, I've overslept. I should have left for work an hour ago.

She climbed out of bed, feeling an ache between her legs that caused her to look down. In horror, she gasped as she noticed bite marks on her inner thighs and scratches on her breasts. Her stomach lurched, as she realised that what had happened last night couldn't have been a dream. These were not the markings someone made to themselves when asleep. Her first thought was James, as she remembered he was returning home that evening and how would she be able to explain this? She looked like she had been attacked but knew he wouldn't see it that way. She had to figure out a way to explain what had happened, but who would believe she had been violated by an unseen force in her bed? Her husband certainly wouldn't. She got under the shower and let the hot water cascade over her, soothing her bruises, and washing away the touch of whoever – or whatever was still lingering on her skin.

4

Arriving at work an hour later, Anna made her way swiftly to her desk and sat down, hoping her lateness would go unnoticed.

"Anna, what are you doing here? You were needed in court today, don't you remember?"

Frank appeared next to her desk, holding a bundle of papers and a coffee mug that looked like it hadn't been washed in weeks, much like the owner. He was her boss and a rather leering one at that. Middle aged and overweight, having let himself go since his wife left him for another woman two years ago.

He was standing uncomfortably close to Anna, and she was hit with the unpleasant aroma of stale cigarettes, coffee, and sweat. She couldn't be sure if Frank just smelled worse than usual that day, or if her sense of smell was heightened but, either way, it turned her stomach.

Go fuck yourself, Frank, she thought to herself.

"Shit…The McKenzie case. I'm so sorry. I overslept. I'm not feeling great today, I shouldn't even be here," she said, trying to sound apologetic.

Resting a rough, nicotine-stained hand on her shoulder, Frank moved closer.

"Something seems off with you Anna. You look different. Are you sure you're okay? I can drive you home if you aren't well and need to rest." He gave her shoulder a squeeze, making her flinch.

"I'm fine, Frank. Honestly," she said stiffly. "I'll see out the morning now I'm here and make myself useful."

The morning went by in a haze for Anna. She couldn't get last night's events out of her head and struggled to concentrate on anything. By lunch time, she had packed up her things and was heading towards the door, when Frank blocked her path.

"Are you sure I can't give you a ride home? You don't look in a good state at all to be driving," he said, moving closer to her. She could smell stale booze and cigarettes on his breath, along with something else she couldn't quite place and didn't really want to know about. She swallowed sharply.

"Frank, please. I'll be fine. I need to call in at the doctor's anyway, so I'll be a while. Women's troubles," she sighed, hoping that would shut him up.

She squeezed past him out the door, aware that he made no effort to move, so he could feel the brush of her breasts against him.

Back in her car, Anna cradled her head in her hands. She still had no idea what she was going to say to James and time was ticking by. He'd be home in a matter of hours, and she knew what he was like the first night home; he'd be expecting sex, and if she didn't give it to him, well, he'd...

Stop. Stop tormenting yourself, Anna. The affair is over, why can't you just let it drop?

Putting the car in gear and driving out of the parking lot, Anna figured the best thing to do would be to tell him the truth. As crazy as it might sound. James knew, as well as she did, that weird things had been happening in the house; she was just there to experience it more, and now things had taken a more sinister turn.

Driving through the sluggish North London traffic, Anna decided to take a detour through Camden Town. She had spent most of her twenties living in this bohemian borough, known for its alternative music scene and culture. Even now, all these years later, she still felt at home there; it was a place where you could lose yourself and be anyone you wanted to be. Feeling a pang of nostalgia as she drove down the main high street, driving past old haunts she used to drink in and watch bands play, she caught sight of a shop she hadn't noticed before. It was a new age shop which looked like it sold the usual crystals and tarot decks, but what struck her about it was the neon sign in the window offering walk-in psychic readings.

Maybe they could shed some light on what is happening to me?

Shops like these reminded her of her childhood. Her grandmother would read tarot and adorn her home with crystals, incense, and all sorts of spiritual paraphernalia. Venturing into these shops, with their sights and smells, transported Anna back to a time when she felt happy and carefree. After her parents were killed in a car crash, Anna had turned her back on the spiritual world. In the days and weeks following their death, she had begged for them to give her a sign that they were there and that there was life beyond death, but she had received nothing. Her grandmother had tried teaching her the old ways, which she had held onto, but any beliefs she may have had were buried alongside her parents. Over time, Anna had become increasingly nihilistic, which in turn had led her to James.

Something inexplicable, which she put down to nostalgia, was calling to her so she pulled up on the street and walked back down towards the shop. As she entered, she was met with the familiar, musky aroma of incense and a warm smile.

"What can I do for you?" asked the shopkeeper as he approached.

He was an elderly man, with what sounded like a Hungarian accent. Anna's mother was Hungarian, so the familiarity immediately put her at ease.

"Oh yes, well, I saw the sign in your window about a reading. I was wondering if I could have one, please?"

"Of course!" he replied with a smile. "My wife, Vadoma, does the readings. I'll go see if she is ready. One moment please. Have a seat just over there." The man gestured to the back of the room, where there was a small sitting area.

He headed through a heavily draped door at the rear of the shop, decorated with rows of amulets. Anna took a moment to wander around the shop for a browse before taking her seat. The air was thick with the scent of Nag

Champa, a sacred incense known for cleansing the energy in a room.

There were rows of crystals in little compartments, which Anna ran her hand over. She felt an inexplicable pull towards the black tourmaline, and when she picked it up it felt hot in her hand, forcing her to drop it. She had some knowledge of crystals, from what she had learned from being around her grandmother, and knew this particular one was to expel negative energy from the body. Her grandmother would fuss over her and press tourmaline into her hand, insisting she carried it whenever she had a headache, as she believed this was a symptom of a spiritual attack or someone wishing her harm. Anna reached again for the tourmaline and quickly popped one in her pocket. She had never stolen anything before, but it caused a rush of adrenaline as she felt the heat radiate from the crystal inside her pocket.

She moved quickly, noticing an occult section a little further along. She picked up a book about black magic and flicked through it. The book fell open to a section on the summoning of spirits and the dangers of demonic possession. There was an image of a naked woman writhing and copulating with an incubus named Belial. The incubus had the body of a man, adorned with serpent tattoos and eyes as black as obsidian. And his smile; she knew that smile from somewhere that she couldn't place.

A sense of unease suddenly washed over her, and she slammed the book shut before placing it back on the shelf. She could feel eyes on her so turned around to see a black cat perched on the counter next to the till. Green eyes stared hard at Anna. She reached out her hand to pet it, but the cat recoiled at her touch, hissing. Shocked by its reaction, Anna went and sat down next to the door, where the shopkeeper had disappeared.

Behind the door, she could hear muffled voices speaking in Hungarian and, for a second, wondered what she was doing there and got to her feet to leave. At that moment, the shopkeeper appeared.

"Vadoma is ready for you now. Please follow me."

5

Anna made her way through the door, the smell of incense growing stronger as she entered the darkened room. In front of her sat an elderly woman with her back turned. She was dressed in black, with a dark laced shawl covering her head, and seated at a small circular table covered with a laced cloth, upon which were a selection of crystals and a deck of tarot cards. The room was lit dimly, with a single tiffany style lamp hanging above the table.

"Come in, please. Take your seat with me at the table." The woman gestured to Anna in a thick accent, raising a gnarled, bejewelled hand.

Anna walked round the table to face the elderly woman and shuddered as she raised her head to face her. The woman's eyes were clouded over and, where there should have been colour, there was only a milky haze. She smiled blindly in Anna's direction and pointed towards the seat opposite her.

"Tell me dear, what has brought you here?" Vadoma asked. As she opened her mouth to speak, Anna caught sight of her teeth which were blackened from decay. The old woman must have been in her late eighties or early nineties but was gnarled, resembling a walking corpse. Age had not been kind to Vadoma. Dressed all in black, her skin was ghostly pale and so thin it was almost translucent. Her wild silver hair was wiry and unkempt under the black veil she had placed over it.

"To be honest, I was hoping you could advise me on something strange that has been happening?" Anna sat down and began to explain the recent events, starting with when they first moved into the house, her erratic changes in behaviour, particularly her increased sexual need, and, more recently, the strange occurrences in the house that had culminated in the sexual attack.

Vadoma remained stone-faced the entire time Anna was talking. Then, without a word, she placed a hand on the tarot cards to her right and started to shuffle. A handful of cards fell out of the deck almost immediately, and she turned them upwards in front of her.

Anna wondered how she could read the cards if she was blind but refrained from asking.

"You may wonder how I can read the cards with the veil covering my eyes. I do not need eyes to see, when I have the spirits to do that for me," Vadoma explained, as if sensing Anna's astonishment.

Brushing her hand over the cards in front of her, Anna could have sworn she saw what little colour remained in the old woman's face drain away.

"You are in great danger, my child," she continued in a low voice. "There is a dark spirit attached to you. A demon who goes by the name of Belial." Vadoma lifted her head to look at Anna with empty eyes.

"I've encountered him once before, long ago. He is a powerful one. If you let him enter you, he will be hard to banish, as he already has laid claim to you," she added.

On hearing these words, Anna's heart began to pound wildly, and she felt a tightness in her throat. She placed her head in her hands to steady herself. It struck her that the name was familiar, as if it belonged to an old acquaintance whom she couldn't place.

The book! That was the page it had fallen open to.

"What does he want from me?" she asked, aghast.

"He is the Lord of Lies. Master of Deception. Some say he is the predecessor of Satan himself, who comes to us as the personification of wickedness and evil. Belial has been in existence for as long as time itself and presents himself as the master of seduction. He will come to you as everything you have ever wanted. If you have problems in your marriage, he will appear to you as your salvation. But be warned, no good will come of this. For once you give in to his temptation, there will be no return. He feeds off sexual energy, like an incubus, and is a profane being, revelling in the pains and pleasure of the flesh."

"But why me? I've never so much as dabbled in anything to do with spirits, so why has he chosen me and what does he want?" Anna cried. A sense of helplessness washed over her, and she began to sob.

"Are you quite sure about that?" Vadoma asked. "He does not come without being invited. You have brought him forth, in one way or another, so you must send him back the same way he came."

The old woman rose to her feet and shuffled over to a cabinet in the corner of the room. She fumbled with a key around her neck before opening it to retrieve an old book and three candles, one red and two white.

Anna couldn't understand how she could have found these items, as the old, blind woman somehow navigated her way back across the room to her.

"The spirits guide my hand," she said, again sensing Anna's thoughts.

"You asked what this dark spirit wants. He wants - well, he wants you. You have given him an invitation. An opening," Vadoma said.

"You must read this book; inside there is a passage which you must follow in order to banish him." The old woman handed her the items, pressing them tightly into Anna's hands that were still shaking in shock.

"Take these with you and do exactly as the book says, tonight. You have no time to lose. I hope we will not need to meet each other again," she concluded solemnly in Hungarian, as if a mutual understanding of their shared heritage had passed between the two women.

6

Anna left the shop in disbelief at what she had been told. The words rang in her head; a spirit attachment? Worse, a demon? Her thoughts were consumed with worry as to how this could have happened and how she would explain it to James. She knew she only had a few hours before he would return from his trip, so she needed to get back and do what Vadoma had instructed. As she passed Highgate Cemetery, she was struck again with the thought of the curse she had uttered. Had that been what had started all this? She remembered not being able to shake off the feeling that she was being followed on the way home, and a chill passed through her as she considered the implications of what she might have brought upon herself. For that had started the chain of events. Had she in some way ended up cursing herself rather than James?

She drove home in a state of shock, casting furtive glances at the items next to her on the passenger seat. This was London 2023, there was no such thing as demonic possession, surely. That was the stuff of nightmares, of Hollywood movies. Not something which would happen to her. However, she wasn't prepared to take any chances, knowing there was something foul at play, so would do whatever it took to rid herself of it.

Upon returning home, the coldness of the house struck her as she walked in the front door. Shivering, she turned the heating on, although she knew it would make little difference. She set the items out on the kitchen table and opened the book. It was an ancient looking, leather-bound grimoire decorated with an array of strange and intricate symbols Anna was unfamiliar with. Vadoma had earmarked the passage Anna would need to read aloud as part of her incantation. As Anna opened the book, and inspected the delicate pages, she felt a darkness come over her, as if something inside of her was recoiling at what was written. The text was faint and in a language she could not understand but, after reciting it in her head several times, she felt confident enough to speak it aloud; she did not want to get this wrong.

The instructions were clear. She was to position herself inside a chalk circle along with the candles. Her name and Belial's were to be written on the white candles and the word 'love' on the red candle. She was to hold them in her hand and visualise them becoming the thing they represented. She then had to tie the candles together and light them before reciting the spell from the book:

Venti cinque carte siete!
Venti cinque diavoli diventerete,
Diventerete, Anderete
Nel'corpo, nel'sanquenell'anima,
Nell sentimenti del corpo;
Del mio amante non posso vivere,
Non passa stare nebere,
Ne mangiare ne
Ne con uonmini ne con donne non passa Favellare
Finche ala pota dicasa mia
Non viene picchiare!

After reciting this passage, she was to sever the rope that bound the candles together and blow out the red one. The next instruction was to visualise the breaking of the bond before separating the remaining candles and snuffing them out.

Just as Anna had finished drawing the circle on the kitchen floor, and was sitting inside ready to begin, she heard a car pull up on the driveway. James was home. She didn't have time to pack all this away, as he would be walking in the door any second. She scrambled to her feet and threw the book inside her bag, just as he entered. She turned to face him with a look of panic as he stood looking at her and down at the candles in astonishment.

"What's going on here? I leave you for one week, and I come home to find you casting spells in the kitchen? What are these?" he said, bending down to pick up the inscribed candles.

"James, listen. I can explain. There's a good reason for this, but I'm going to need you to sit down and hear me out," Anna pleaded. Trembling, she gestured for him to sit down. Her mind was racing as she tried to piece together the recent events that had led them to where they now stood. Underneath her clothes, the bruises throbbed, and she took a deep breath before starting to speak. When she got to the part where she described the sexual attack, her voice faltered and she dropped her gaze, unable to look her husband in the eye.

He stared at her in shock as she lifted her clothes to show him the marks on her skin.

"Wait, you are telling me a demon did this to you? Anna, you must think I'm fucking stupid," he shouted. "Seems a little convenient that all of this happens while I'm away, and when I return, you are covered in bruises. It looks to me like rough sex. You just didn't want me to find out about your lover, did you?" He stood up angrily, slamming his fist down on the table.

"You are going to tell me who you have been fucking," he roared. Whoever he is, I'm going to kill him for fucking my wife. Give me his name, now!"

"James, please! I'm telling you the truth, why can't you believe me?" Anna begged. "Can't you see there is something wrong with this house? We should never have moved here - there's something evil here and it's latched onto me!"

"Something evil?" he sneered. "A house can't be evil, it's just a building. A shell. People are evil, Anna, but you can't pin this on a house. You're just never satisfied, are you? I work my arse off to provide for you and buy us a house like this. If we had to depend on you, we'd still be living hand to mouth in a shitty one-bed flat."

Anna's eyes welled up with tears as she listened to her husband's cruel words. Of course this was all her fault. Everything always was. She knew that when James had a temper, there was no getting him out of it. He stormed out of the house, slamming the door behind him, leaving her alone once more with only her disturbed thoughts.

7

James sat in the car and gripped the steering wheel so tightly that his knuckles turned white. He was shaking with anger, not just at the thought of someone else having access to his wife, but that Anna could lie to his face like that. He'd had his dalliances with other women but had told himself he deserved them. He worked hard and the affairs had meant nothing, just allowing him to let off some steam. His wife had been so uptight until recently, after all. Anna had everything so easy. He was the main provider, she wanted for nothing, so why couldn't she be grateful? She always had to mess everything up.

He looked at himself in the rear-view mirror. He was still handsome enough, what was it she was looking for in other men that he didn't have? He still had all of his own hair, plenty of it in fact. Dark curls, with a light sprinkling of grey at the temples; his beard also showed his age but women liked that, didn't they? His pale blue eyes were the physical feature that Anna said she had noticed first. They seemed to change colour with his mood; more often they were blue, but at other times they were grey. Today they resembled an angry sea. James was in good shape too; he worked out at the gym most evenings before returning home. He found that the afterwork gym crowd had the best pickings of women. He knew he got many an admiring glance, when he pumped the iron, and he thrived off the attention.

Driving into Soho, he crawled through the red-light district. He knew what he needed to do to make himself feel better. There was a little walk-up place he knew of where the girls were clean and cheap. He needed to take his frustration out somewhere.

Parking up close by, where he knew he wouldn't be spotted by anyone, he headed down a back street towards the flat. He hadn't visited it for years, but when he knocked on the door it was answered by an old, familiar face.

"Oh, it's you. It's been a long time. Which one are you here for?" the woman asked.

"Angie. Is she still here?"

"Yes. She'll need a few minutes. Wait inside," the woman said. Her face was tired and drawn, looking much older than her years, as this was not a kind lifestyle for these women. Her badly rooted hair was bleached a cheap shade of bottle blonde, and she bore the faint scars of track marks on her flaccid arms. Once prostitutes reached a certain age, their desirability waned, so they often became the *maid*, who met the clients at the door on behalf of the girls.

James stepped inside the dark hallway. It felt damp, and the air was thick with the smell of stale cigarette smoke. The carpet was threadbare, and there was no furniture in the hallway, aside from a single chair, which James sat down on while the woman headed upstairs.

A few minutes later, she returned and gestured for James to head on up.

"She's ready for you now. Second door on the left," she said brusquely, handing him a condom. "Make sure you wear it."

He threw some crumpled notes at her outstretched hands and headed upstairs. The floorboards creaked heavily under his feet, and the carpet felt sticky underfoot.

He knocked on the door, and Angie opened it.

"Well hello stranger, it's been a while," she said in a voice ravaged by too many cigarettes, forcing a smile. "You missed me then?"

The woman was wearing a black satin kimono which was open, exposing red laced underwear underneath. Angie was in her late twenties but looked older. She was probably getting close to the age where she would have to retire soon, and her price reflected that. It was why James had chosen her; if he was going to spend his money on prostitutes, they had to be cheap. Her French bob was dyed black, severe against her pale skin, but her red lips brought colour to an otherwise drained looking face. Mascara was smeared under sad, tired eyes, as if she had recently been crying and then hastily wiped them. If anyone knew how to paint a smile on, it was a Soho prostitute.

The room was sparsely furnished. It had a double bed with satin sheets, a sink, and an old-fashioned looking dresser adorned with cheap perfume and makeup. James wondered how often the sheets were washed. Net curtains hung loosely at the window, the bright city lights and noise streaming through them. This was not a room for sleeping in, he thought.

Angie led him over to the bed.

"What's it going to be then?" she asked, with feigned enthusiasm. Her teeth were nicotine stained and her face looked sunken, from where she was missing a couple of molars on the left side. She didn't look as good as he remembered.

Without a word, James threw her back onto the bed. He stood over her, kicking her legs apart with his feet, as he wrenched her knickers down.

"Not so rough, please!" Angie begged. "You hurt me last time, remember? I couldn't work for days afterwards."

She gasped as James tossed the unused condom aside and forced himself inside her, raw, having hastily unbuckled his trousers and pulled them and his boxer shorts down. His pelvis thrust aggressively against her, making her cry out as he grunted heavily. He wrapped his hands around her throat to stifle her cries, watching her face turn red from asphyxiation. Just as he was about to come, he took his hands off Angie's throat and grabbed a handful of her hair, pulling her up towards him as she struggled for breath.

"How do you like this, you fucking slut?" he growled.

"Stop! Please…you're hurting me!" Angie cried.

"I'll stop when I'm finished," he spat before throwing her over onto her front. He pounded into her aggressively for several more minutes before finally releasing himself inside her.

Dropping her back down on the bed like a discarded ragdoll, Angie was a quivering mess. She lay there, shaking in shock, unable to move as tears ran silently down her face.

"Please…just leave," she whimpered.

Without looking at her or saying another word, James pulled his trousers up, turned on his heel, and slammed the door behind him.

He didn't notice the flame-haired woman sitting in her car at the end of the street, watching him leave the brothel. He didn't see when she stepped out of the car, spurred on by the voice in her head to walk up to the front door and enquire where her husband had just been.

8

It was a little after midnight, and several beers and whiskey chasers later, when James returned home. He made his way upstairs and could hear Anna murmuring in her sleep. She appeared restless, and the bedroom felt colder than usual, accompanied by an odd smell. He decided to go and sleep in the spare room instead, so as not to be disturbed by her.

He had only been asleep for a couple of hours when he woke suddenly. Anna was standing at the side of the bed, staring at him, naked and muttering something under her breath that he could not make sense of. Assuming that she must be sleepwalking, he got out of bed and guided her back to the bedroom.

James gasped when he entered the room. It was a mess. Everything had been overturned. Sheets ripped off the bed, drawers emptied, and clothes from the wardrobe strewn all over the floor. He shook Anna to wake her up.

"Anna! Wake up, what the fuck has happened in here?" he yelled, slapping her in the face to rouse her.

As if snapping out of a trance, she regained her composure and stared around the room.

"I – I have no idea? I had a bad dream, but I don't remember anything" she said, perplexed, cradling her sore cheek.

"I don't know what's got into you, but you need to tidy this up and sort yourself out," James snarled, slamming the door behind him, leaving Anna speechless and confused.

The following morning, Anna woke with a headache.

As she walked down the stairs, she heard James moving around in the kitchen. She was angry with him, after following him to the brothel yesterday, but her face gave nothing away. She understood enough to know she couldn't let on about knowing where he had been. He needed to be taught a lesson, even though she wasn't sure yet what that would be. The voice in her head had been getting louder and more affirmative, guiding her in what she should do.

As she entered the room, she feigned a look of confusion and weariness. James turned around, shooting her a disgusted look.

"I want that mess cleaned up by the time I get home tonight," he said, scowling at her.

Hurt him. Do it.

She felt a fury rise inside her and strode over to the island to retrieve her handbag. Without saying a word, she pulled out her cigarettes and lit one, much to the disgust of her husband.

"Since when have you started smoking in the house? Is this something else you've been doing with your lover?" he snapped.

Anna took a long drag from the Marlboro and walked towards him. Looking him dead in the eye, she plunged the cigarette down onto his bare arm and held it there, gripping it with her other hand as he shrieked in pain and tried to pull away.

"FUCK, Anna!"

"You will never, ever talk to me like a piece of shit again. Do you understand?" She spoke in a low, commanding voice, her eyes darkening as she held his gaze.

As she looked at him, she could see a flicker of something resembling fear in his face. She had never stood up for herself before and seeing him flinch away from her filled her with satisfaction. She held onto his arm, squeezing it with a newfound strength she didn't know she had. She wondered if she twisted it enough, whether it would break.

"Anna, stop! That fucking hurts!"

She eventually let go and smiled. It was a smile that asserted her dominance over him.

James retreated from her, cradling his arm.

"I don't know what's up with you Anna, but I think you need help." He hurried out of the kitchen and left the house for work.

As the front door slammed shut, Anna took her seat at the kitchen table. She felt different but couldn't fathom how or why. She ran her hand down over her black robe, enjoying the feel of her curves beneath the silk material and, as she did so, felt something inside of her stir. She felt different. Slipping out of her negligee, she relished her nakedness, allowing her fingers to trace over the heavy swell of her breasts before making their way down between her legs. She slid them inside with ease, enjoying the wetness of her folds. Feeling the tension in her body begin to subside, she kept her fingers inside while she circled her slick clit with her thumb, her breathing quickening as she increased the rhythm. It felt different this time, and her hand grew numb, as if someone or something had control of her hand and was relentlessly fucking her. Closing her eyes, she threw her head back and gasped loudly as the orgasm washed over her in luxurious waves. Invisible hands gripped her throat, holding it in place, as her hand brought her to a shuddering climax.

It's you. It's always been you.

It was at that moment, from behind closed eyes, that she saw him.

She saw him in a vision, standing behind her. The stranger from the bar. Except he was the Devil himself, of that she was certain. Tall, well dressed in a tailored suit, dark hair streaked with grey, and black eyes to match. Grey stubble adorned a chiselled jawline with a face so handsome. Anna had never laid eyes on anything so perfect. He had the appearance of a man in his early fifties, but she sensed that he was as old as time itself. His hands were clasped around her throat, as if commanding her body to respond to his request and, as she gave herself over to the ecstatic ripples running through her body, he smiled darkly.

I've been waiting for you Anna. Give yourself over to me.

Yes.

She opened her eyes upon saying that word and, in doing so, felt him retract. She was alone again in the room yet felt oddly at ease with what had just happened. As she regained her composure, she glanced at the clock above the door.

Now to deal with the other one.

Anna took a long shower and picked her most flattering blouse and pencil skirt before heading to the car.

Battling through the traffic to the south side of town, she reached work a little after nine. She walked into the office, red lipstick freshly applied, hair perfectly styled, and whether it was her new perfume or pheromones, she turned the heads of everyone she passed. Frank, however, was already waiting for her at her desk with a face like thunder.

"What time do you call this, Anna? A word in my office, now," he ordered, glaring at her whilst also shooting a cursory glance over her body.

Following Frank into his office, she felt the burning rage come over her again. He closed the door behind them, blocking her exit.

"Listen, if there are problems at home, you should know you can talk to me?"

She felt an incessant fury rising inside of her. It was a rage that had simmered below the surface for months, whenever Frank tried to get her alone, but one which, until now, she had always managed to suppress. Now, however, the voice was telling her not to repress it any longer.

Let's teach him a lesson he won't forget.

His tone had changed now they were alone. He placed a hand on her shoulder, and she could smell the lurid desire rolling off him. Beads of perspiration made his greasy ginger hair cling to his forehead. It made her stomach churn, but she knew what he wanted. If she sucked his cock, all this would be forgotten.

"You know what I want," he said, moving in closer, his stale cigarette breath making her recoil. "We can make this little problem go away."

The anger bubbling inside her erupted, and she shot out her hand, grabbing Frank forcibly by the balls.

"Yes Frank, I do know what you want. We all know what you want," she hissed, grappling at his belt, forcibly ignoring the odour plaguing her nostrils.

Pushing him back against the door, she got down on her knees and pulled his trousers and saggy underpants down, exposing his cock that was already hard and throbbing.

She could sense the entity inside her stir as she wrapped her lips around his erection. As she raised her eyes to look at him, Frank gasped. Her eyes had turned to black saucers, and her face became distorted as she smiled cruelly up at him.

He staggered, and tried to pull himself free, but she held him firmly between her teeth as she bit down hard.

Through her clenched jaw, a demonic voice emanated from inside her.

"How do you like this, Frank? Wasn't this what you wanted?" it mocked. "Is this how your wife used to suck your cock?"

Anna was foaming at the mouth, and her eyes started to roll back into her head as, all the while, the voice emanating from her laughed.

Reeling from the pain, Frank yelled for help as he banged on the door, trying to wrench himself free. Just as it was flung open, Anna's jaw released, and she fell back from him.

Frank's secretary stood in the doorway aghast. Anna was lying on the floor, dazed, while Frank stood over her with his trousers down, his flaccid penis on full display.

By now a small crowd had gathered, as they had heard the commotion coming from inside Frank's office. Some looked aghast, while others stifled a giggle.

"This isn't what it looks like!" Frank shouted as he wrestled with his trousers. "She attacked me, the woman is insane. Get her out of here!"

Frank's secretary rushed over to tend to Anna, who had regained her composure and was quickly back on her feet. She forced her way past the group congregated in the doorway and grabbed her bag, before fleeing the office. She didn't know where she would go, but she knew she couldn't stay there.

Her mind raced as she bundled her belongings into the car and sped off out of the car park. What had come over her? She knew what she had done to Frank, but it hadn't felt like she was in control of her actions. She had felt possessed, as if the thing inside of her had taken over and used her body as a vessel.

She knew there was only one person who understood. It was time to pay another visit to Vadoma.

9

As Anna pulled up to the shop, she noticed the shutters had been pulled down. A handwritten sign was attached to the front door.

CLOSED UNTIL FURTHER NOTICE.

An uneasy feeling came over Anna. Something wasn't right. There was a phone number on the shop's signage, so she pulled out her phone and called the number.

It rang several times before a voice answered.

"Hello?" It sounded like the gentleman she had met yesterday.

"Oh, hello. It's Anna. I visited yesterday and had a reading with Vadoma. I was hoping to speak with her again please, if possible?"

There was a long pause.

"I'm very sorry but that won't be possible." he said, flatly. "There was an accident last night, shortly after you left the shop. Vadoma is dead."

"What? How?!" Anna asked. A feeling of dread washed over her, and her head began to pound. She felt sick to her stomach.

"She fell down a flight of stairs and broke her neck," the man said. "She had a feeling you would return and had gone down to the basement to retrieve something she thought might have been of use to you but missed her footing and fell."

She shouldn't have interfered.

Anna struggled to suppress the intrusive voice in her head, which was plaguing her mind increasingly by the day. She was having difficulty separating her own thoughts from the rogue voice inside her.

"I'm so sorry. I feel terrible," Anna said. "I can't help but feel responsible for this."

"It's not your fault." he answered after another pause, but Anna could tell by his tone that he didn't mean that.

"I don't mean to sound insensitive, but may I ask what it was that she wanted me to have?"

"It was an amulet. Vadoma believed it might have offered you some protection. Come by the shop this evening around seven, and I will give it to you. It makes sense for you to have it, then perhaps my wife hasn't died in vain."

He hung up, and Anna was left wondering what this all meant. Vadoma had known she would return and had wanted to help her. What were the chances of her having a fatal accident; it was as if something or someone had stopped her? A chill ran through Anna as she turned and headed back to her car.

With Vadoma dead, who will be able to help me now?

She spent the rest of the afternoon driving around town aimlessly, calling at a nearby cafe for something to eat but all she could do was stare at the food in front of her for she had no appetite. She hadn't wanted to go home, as she wasn't yet ready to face James, and just wanted to be around other people.

Seven that evening came, and Anna returned to the shop. Her headache had worsened, and she felt as though a mist was being pulled over her eyes in an attempt to draw her away from the shop. She walked up to the front door, despite the voice in her head coaxing her to return to the car and leave.

All this would be so much easier for you Anna if you simply allowed me to take control. Let me in.

The door was locked but she could see a light on at the back of the shop so she pressed the buzzer. A few moments later, the door opened, and she was greeted by Vadoma's husband.

He gestured for her to come inside, then shut the door softly behind them.

"Please wait here, I'll go fetch it," he said, casting sad eyes over Anna.

He looked like he had aged overnight. The sparkle she had noticed in his eyes yesterday had gone, replaced by a heavy tiredness. Drained. It was to be expected, given he had just lost his wife, and Anna's heart went out to him.

"Thank you for agreeing to meet with me," she said. "I'm sorry, I don't even know your name."

"It's Jozsef," he answered. "I don't want Vadoma to have died for nothing, so it's important to me that you have this. It's what she would have wanted."

He shuffled through to the back room and returned a few moments later with a small black box clutched close to his chest.

With trembling hands, he carefully set the box down on the counter, close to the door, before opening it. Inside was a silver pendant, tarnished with age, and adorned with intricate inscriptions. Anna reached to pick it up, but Jozsef blocked her hand.

"This amulet may look just like any other pendant, but it holds great power and must be treated with respect," he said sternly. "It has been handed down through Vadoma's family for generations to offer protection against the evilest of spirits. We can't be sure if it will work to dispel this entity, but you have Roma blood running through your veins so we must try."

Anna looked at him, perplexed. "How do you know about my family?" she asked. "My maternal grandmother was Hungarian Roma, but I don't recall having mentioned it."

"Vadoma knew. You forget how her spirits told her everything. You should have been easy for her to read, but there was a darkness surrounding you which she could not penetrate."

On hearing his words, Anna shuddered. The voice inside her laughed. A cruel, mocking sound unlike one she had heard before. She was desperate to drown out the sound of it and raised her hands to her ears to silence it.

"STOP IT!" she yelled out loud.

"What is wrong?"

Flushed, Anna lowered her hands. "Nothing, sorry. It's just, well… you wouldn't understand."

Jozsef stared at her in concern before reaching inside the box to retrieve the pendant. Unclasping it, he held it to Anna's neck and secured it in place.

Immediately, she felt heat radiate from it and gasped as the metal scorched her skin.

"It burns! I can't wear this!" she cried.

"You must," warned Jozsef. "It will settle in time, but you must allow it to work its power. Now go home and rest. You will need it."

10

As Anna drove home, the burning from the pendant subsided to a dull throb. She dreaded the conversation she knew she would be having with James. Her heart was in her throat as she pulled onto the driveway and saw his car already there. He would be wondering where she was and, no doubt, that would make him even more angry. How would she explain losing her job? Feigning illness would buy her some time, but it would not be a long-term solution; he would find out soon enough.

Closing the front door behind her, the house felt eerily quiet. No lights were on downstairs, and there was no sign of James anywhere. Entering the living room, she saw discarded beer cans strewn over the coffee table, along with a half-emptied bottle of whiskey and James collapsed on the sofa in a sound sleep. She thought it best not to wake him, for his temper could be unpredictable when fuelled with whiskey, so she left the room and made her way upstairs to bed.

Halfway up the stairs, however, she paused as a dark thought came over her. She turned on her heel and made her way back down the stairs and into the kitchen. It was as if someone else was in control of her body as she made her way over to the knife rack on the counter. She picked out the largest kitchen knife and passed back through the hallway, and into the living room, where she stood over James, peering down at him asleep. He looked so peaceful.

We need to teach him a lesson he won't forget.

She lifted the knife to his throat and traced it lightly across the skin, nicking it slightly.

Do it. It'll be quick. He won't feel a thing.

The sight of his blood, seeping from the small cut she had made on his throat, shook Anna out of her trance, and she gasped as she came to, dropping the knife from her hands.

What am I doing? This is wrong!

With a sob, she fled the living room and hurried upstairs, throwing herself onto the bed as she let the tears flow.

She cried into her pillow, desperate to drown out the cacophony of noise inside her head and eventually fell into a slumber but was awoken a few hours later by the familiar scratching and a penetrating chill in the room. Anna sat up and glanced at the clock. It was three in the morning. She could see her breath as she exhaled; something felt wrong. There was a heavy energy in the room which felt as though it was creeping closer, enveloping her in a thick fold of darkness.

An invisible force threw her back onto the bed, pinned down and unable to move. Her chest felt compressed, as if something was crushing it, and her limbs stiffened. She felt a stirring deep within her, something parasitic, a foreign body moving inside her, taking possession.

"Stop! Please! What is it you want from me?" she cried into the darkness, wrestling against the unseen entity which had her pinned to the bed.

She then became aware of a dark mass taking shape above her, and a disembodied voice above her growled.

Give yourself over to me, Anna. Do not try to resist me. You already know the power I have over you and what I am capable of.

Unable to control her body, her legs parted, and she felt an overwhelming force push itself inside her. One part of her remained terrified, yet the other was aroused by the sensation. Closing her eyes, she thought back to the face she had seen in her vision the day before in the kitchen. The dark eyes, which had penetrated her to the very core, and the knowing smile that had brought her to a heady climax.

You see me, don't you. Now give yourself to me, completely. Allow me to claim you as my own and all your troubles will cease. You just need to let me in. Say it. Say you belong to me.

Anna could feel the throbbing between her legs intensify and, as she allowed her body to erupt into orgasm, ripped the burning pendant from her throat, letting the entity consume her as she finally gave herself over to it.

"Yes," she moaned, putting up no further resistance. "Fuck me like this, and I'll be yours."

It was at that moment of release, the image of man transformed to that of a beast. A hideous monster loomed over her, its mouth twisting into an unnatural smile that stretched all the way across its face. Weeping sores covered its body, oozing foul smelling, viscous fluid. Purple veins bulged from black, amphibious skin, and to Anna's horror, as she looked down, she could see another gaping mouth beginning to protrude from its bloated stomach, its black tongue extending, dripping saliva over her as the mouth gnawed blindly at the air. From the creature's mouth, she heard a cacophony of wailing emanating from deep within its belly, as if harbouring trapped souls of the damned.

That was the last thing she remembered before everything went black.

11

James woke a little after ten in the living room, with a thumping headache. He couldn't remember how much he had drunk the previous night, but if his head was anything to go by, he knew it had been too much. He cast a bleary eye over the coffee table in front of him and the empty whiskey bottle. He had no recollection of getting home; the last thing he recalled was downing shots in a Soho dive bar.

He stretched and got to his feet, hearing something metallic clatter to the floor. His neck ached and, upon rubbing it, he noticed blood on his fingers. It was then that he noticed the knife at his feet, which must have fallen from the sofa.

He couldn't hear any movement upstairs, and it was only as he stepped out into the hallway that he heard a creak from above. It was slow and repetitive, as if someone, or something, was rocking back and forth over the floorboards.

James raced up the stairs to confront Anna about why he had woken up with an injured neck, convinced she must have been trying to scare him, given her recent erratic behaviour but stopped in his tracks as he felt the temperature plummet upon reaching the landing. The anger he felt was suddenly replaced by a deep sense of unease. Gripping the bannister, he peered down the mouth of the dark corridor before going any further. Something didn't feel right.

"Anna?" he called into the void.

The creaking stopped.

"Answer me, goddammit. Don't make me come in there," he shouted.

Creeping warily down the corridor, he put his ear to the bedroom door. He could make out shuffling coming from inside, as if something heavy was being dragged across the floor.

He then heard what sounded like muffled laughter and felt his anger rise again, as he cast his mind back to what Anna had told him about the mystery bruises she had fervently denied were from rough sex.

She must have a man in there.

He threw open the bedroom door, in a fit of rage, but what he saw in front of him couldn't be further from what he had imagined.

Anna was huddled, naked and bloody, in a corner of the room. Her skin was covered in scratches, and she rocked back and forth on the spot with a manic look in her eyes, which were fixed on the opposite corner of the room. She was chanting something incoherently. James recognised it as sounding similar to what he had heard her mutter when he had woken to find her by the side of his bed.

"Anna! Fuck! What have you done to yourself?!" He rushed over to her and tried to pull her to her feet but, upon touching her, was thrown back across the room by an unseen force. Anna turned to face him, roaring, her mouth expanding in grotesque contortion.

"APHR A' LEPHUMAKH!" she shrieked, leaping onto all fours as if to pounce.

Her face was horrifically distorted in a grimace that James couldn't be certain was one of pain or delirium. Her blue eyes were now black craters, filled with pure evil. They were the Devil's eyes. As she rocked on her heels, glaring at James, she tilted her head to the side and her mouth twisted into a bloody, toothless smile that stretched in a grotesque fashion across her face. James noticed, with horror, that she had wrenched her own teeth out, now scattered about the floor around her.

"Here he is," she snarled in a deep, masculine voice. "Always one to make an entrance. How nice to be acquainted. I've been having such fun with your wife, while you have been away." Anna threw her head back and laughed scornfully.

Dumbstruck, James edged backwards towards the door. Beads of sweat were running down his face and, as he opened his mouth to speak, no words would come. His body was shaking in fear as he stared at his wife in all her distortion. He knew she had been unwell, but harming herself to this degree, it was as if she was possessed. But that couldn't be possible, there had to be another explanation.

Scrambling to his feet, he fled the room, crashing the door behind him. Anna needed medical assistance; of that he could be sure. Running downstairs, he could still hear her laughing maniacally from the bedroom as he hunted for his phone.

His fingers fumbled over the keypad; they were shaking so much.

"999, what is your emergency?" the operator asked calmly.

"Ambulance, please - it's for my wife," he cried. "She's in a bad way. I found her upstairs, she has been cutting herself to shreds, and I think she's having some sort of mental breakdown!"

"Okay, sir. Can I take your name please and where you are calling from?"

"Sure, it's James Hayward. My wife's name is Anna. We're at 66 Primrose Gardens, Belsize Park."

"Thank you, Mr Hayward. Do you believe there is an immediate threat to your wife's life?"

"She has lost a lot of blood and has pulled her own teeth out, I'd call that a pretty serious fucking threat to life, wouldn't you?" he yelled down the phone.

"Calm down, sir. We'll have an ambulance dispatched to your address immediately. In the meantime, I need to ask you, providing she is of no threat, to approach her and make sure the area around her is secure from anything she could harm herself further with. The paramedics will be with you soon and will take over from there."

James hung up, throwing the phone down on the kitchen table. It was silent upstairs; the laughing had stopped, yet he was afraid to approach her again for fear of what she might do to him. She had looked at him in such a scornful, mocking way, as if all the sins he had committed were written over him for her to see. He wasn't going to be humiliated like that and, as much as he hated to admit it, he was scared of her. He cast his mind back to the cigarette incident the other day, when she had set out to intentionally harm him and instinctively raised a hand to his bloodied neck. The look in her eyes had shown the degree of hate she had for him, but her behaviour today had been nothing short of psychotic. She was sick and needed help.

Twenty minutes later, the ambulance crew arrived, and James led them with trepidation upstairs to the bedroom. He explained what he had found, lying that he had remained with her after making the call. He opened the bedroom door with caution, stepping aside to let the crew enter the room, fearful for what they might find behind the door.

He followed them cautiously. Anna was back in a catatonic state, rocking back and forth on the spot. One of the paramedics had approached her and was crouched down, holding her hand and speaking gently.

"Anna, can you hear me? Squeeze my hand if you can hear me," she asked in a soothing manner.

"I couldn't get any sense out of her," said James. "This is how I found her earlier, before she was about to attack me."

"Did she attack you, Mr Hayward?" the paramedic asked.

"No, but she looked like she was about to. She got very aggressive and was babbling all sorts of nonsense. I couldn't make any sense of it."

"Okay, I think we need to get your wife moved. I can see she's caused a great deal of harm to herself, and she needs to be taken somewhere safe. We'll take her to the hospital to get her checked over properly. Are you okay to follow us there, Mr Hayward?"

"Yes, yes of course. Is she going to be okay?"

"Physically, she seems to be stable, but it's not my place to make that judgement call; she needs to be clinically assessed by the psychiatric team. You say she made advances, as if to attack you, so she could well be a danger to others as well as herself. The best place for your wife right now is at the hospital. Come on, let's get her moved."

The crew wrapped Anna in a blanket and guided her to the ambulance. As James stood by, and watched her leave the room, she turned to look at him, as if momentarily released from her unresponsive state, and smiled darkly. James shuddered and took a step back, allowing them to pass. Was she really ill, he wondered, or was this all a defiant and extreme act for attention?

It didn't take long for them to reach the hospital. Anna was helped out of the ambulance and taken straight through to the Accident and Emergency Department for assessment. James was directed to the waiting area, where he was informed that a doctor would come and find him once they had an update on Anna's status.

Minutes passed, then hours, before finally an exhausted male doctor emerged, asking for a Mr Hayward. James stood up to make himself known, and the doctor called him over.

"Good evening, Mr Hayward, apologies for keeping you waiting," he said, unsmiling. "Let us go somewhere a little more private where we can talk."

"When can I see my wife?" James asked angrily. "I've been waiting hours."

"I'm afraid that won't be possible just yet, Mr Hayward," advised the doctor as he led them into a meeting room off the main waiting area. "Your wife has sustained a number of injuries, the nature of which concerns us. Our assessment shows she has lost all her teeth, and the markings over her body are most alarming, as we cannot see how she could have inflicted these on herself. Lastly, and most seriously, the bruising she has incurred would indicate a sexual assault may have taken place."

"What?! Are you sure? This is madness. Sexual assault? You mean to say my wife has been raped?" James shouted.

"I'm very sorry Mr Hayward. I'm afraid our initial assessment does suggest that, but she is unresponsive to any sort of questioning, so we'd like to move her to a psychiatric unit, where the mental health specialists can assess her further and take the necessary next steps."

James sat down, shaking his head in disbelief. He couldn't believe this was happening. He hadn't believed Anna, when she had told him about an attack. As for all the cuts over her body, and her teeth having been pulled out, how could this possibly be explained? He knew what the doctor was thinking; he was a suspect of course. First on the scene to find her in this state, he knew how these things went. Poor, unsuspecting Anna, the dutiful wife everyone would feel sorry for. He felt the rage stir up again and swallowed it back down. He knew he had to be careful how he responded to this, as fingers would now be pointing at him.

"Okay, Doctor," he said calmly. "Yes, of course. Whatever is best for my wife. I just can't believe this is happening." He forced the tears to well up in his eyes before wiping them away dramatically.

"Go home, Mr Hayward. We'll make the necessary calls to find a unit that has a bed available for her, and we will be in touch."

James rose to his feet, extending an arm towards the doctor as if to shake his hand. The doctor looked at him without reciprocation.

"We'll be in touch," he repeated coldly before leaving the room.

12

Anna woke later that night. She looked around the room, unsure of where she was. Everything looked so clinical. Then it dawned on her.

What am I doing here? I need to get out of this place!

She pulled at the wires attached to her, ripping out the catheter in the process. Her head felt like it had been crushed in a vice, and she was having trouble focusing, as if a thin veil had been placed over her eyes; she felt nauseous. Her mouth felt funny too, and she ran her tongue around her mouth, realising then why it felt so odd, before letting out a blood curdling scream.

Two nurses came running into the room almost immediately and fought to pin Anna back down onto the bed. She was resisting with all her strength in an attempt to fend them off, alarms sounding from where they had alerted the team. The last thing Anna saw was a doctor in a white coat walking into the room and calmly telling her everything was going to be okay before she felt a sharp sting in her arm, and everything went black.

As Anna slipped into sedation, she could feel herself trying to scream but no sound would come. It was as if her body no longer belonged to her, and she was trapped inside a vessel. She felt like she was being pulled in different directions by invisible hands. Hands which clawed at her, molesting her. She was surrounded by unseen forces but could find no way out. She could see nothing, only black void. But she felt him. She may not have been able to see him, but there was no mistaking his presence. It was all-consuming and mocking. In her blind, helpless state she heard his laugh. It wasn't the same laugh she had heard from him before; this one felt colder. More scornful. It was then she realised what she had done, causing her to cry silent, helpless tears.

Why?

You made it so easy for me, Anna. You invited me in. All of this is your own making. You called to me that day in the cemetery. Oh, how you wanted me then. You begged to be wanted. Desired. You entered into a contract with me, one where you promised to give yourself over unconditionally. Then you spoke those words to me. *A legnagyobb kívánságod lesz a legrosszabb rémálmod.* May their wish soon become their worst nightmare. Well, Anna, with my help you have become both the wish and the worst nightmare.

No! I never wished for it to be like this.

It's too late now, Anna. You made a promise and now you are bound to me. I am inside you and all around you. I am you and you are me, in body and in blood.

13

The next morning Anna was transported to a psychiatric hospital just north of the city in rural Hertfordshire. Radcliffe House was a bleak building, understaffed and in great need of repair. However, all the available funding had already been stretched too thinly across mental health services, so there was none to spare. Anna's room was dreary and windowless, painted a murky shade of green. The only furniture was a railed bed made of steel with restraints in place, if needed. This was a last resort for referrals, as any doctor sending their patients there knew it rarely ended well for them. Rumours circulated that patients were largely neglected and often ended up going increasingly insane from the isolation and lack of adequate care. If they weren't suicidal before being admitted, chances were, the intrusive thoughts would develop after a short stay at Radcliffe.

James had been informed where Anna was being taken and made the journey up the following day to see her. He wanted to make sure he was projecting himself as the caring husband, who was distraught at what had happened to his wife. However, after he had left the hospital, where Anna had been taken the previous day, he had tried to visit Angie again. When he had knocked on the door, it had been the same woman as before who answered, telling him Angie had left town. He had asked for another girl, but she told him in no uncertain terms she had none to offer him before closing the door in his face. He couldn't understand why another girl couldn't be offered in her place; was his cash not good enough? He was oblivious to the visit Anna had made, where a sizeable amount of money had been handed over to buy their cooperation and a threat made that if the door was ever opened to her husband again, they would all be burned in their beds as they slept. He had then roamed the streets of Soho, like a rabid wolf in search of prey to devour, but had ended up in the same sordid bar he always did, lost in a bottle of whiskey.

As he arrived at Radcliffe, James looked up at the imposing building in front of him. It was an eyesore in an otherwise beautiful part of the country. He wondered why anyone would have thought to have built such a monstrosity here. It seemed only fitting it was used to house the mentally ill, for no one of sound mind would willingly set foot in it, he thought. He felt a chill run down him as he walked towards the entrance. It felt like he was being watched from the bleak, dark windows above.

He approached the tired looking reception desk, behind which an equally tired looking receptionist was seated.

"Can I help you?" she asked flatly, without looking up from her screen.

"I was informed my wife was brought here earlier. I'd like to see her please."

"I don't know if you'll be able to see your wife, but I'll let one of the doctors know you are here," she replied, reaching for the telephone. "Name please?"

"James Hayward. My wife is Anna Hayward."

She nodded over towards the seating area for James to wait, which consisted of a handful of weathered chairs, some of which looked like they might collapse if he sat down too quickly. The pale blue leather upholstery groaned as he took his seat. There were no magazines or vending machines, just an empty water dispenser, the murky dregs of which looked like they had been there for months.

A little while later, a doctor came into the reception area to greet James. He looked wired, like he hadn't slept properly in weeks. James knew how that felt.

"Good morning, Mr Hayward. I'm Doctor Lynch. Apologies for keeping you waiting. I'm afraid we've had rather a night of it here. Since your wife was admitted, many of the residents have been a little more, shall we say, lively than usual. It's been all hands-on-deck and sadly we don't have too many of those as it is," he said wearily. "Please follow me, we'll have a chat in my office. Can I offer you a drink?"

"Black coffee would be great, please," James said, his head pounding from the whiskey headache.

Doctor Lynch opened the door to his less than grand office and gestured for James to step inside and take a seat. The office didn't seem much of an improvement from the waiting area, but he was glad to have a coffee in hand at least, despite it being the instant kind that tasted bitter and grainy.

"How is my wife?" he asked, feigning a look of concern.

"Your wife is an interesting case, Mr Hayward. She came to us with a number of physical injuries, of course, but it's the mental ones which are of most concern to us. You see, usually the patient shows some kind of response to the initial assessment, yet your wife shows nothing but apathy, which is unusual given the nature and extent of the injuries she has sustained. We would have expected some sort of resistance to being handled, yet it's almost as if she isn't actually there. Did she show any sort of indication she was unwell prior to this? It's almost unheard of for someone with no history of mental illness to inflict these injuries upon themselves, so we have to assume this was done to her. However, it is of course her response to these injuries, or lack of response, which we are most concerned about here."

James opened his mouth to begin to tell the story of what Anna had told him, but he stopped himself and swallowed. He knew just how ridiculous it sounded, and it would only serve to incriminate him further if he tried to pin these injuries on some sort of supernatural entity.

"No. I had no idea at all," he lied, running a hand over his mouth.

Doctor Lynch studied him intently from across the desk. He glanced at James' left hand and noticed he was not wearing a wedding ring. "Most unusual, indeed," he muttered. "I think it's best we continue to keep your wife under observation for the next few days. Perhaps she may be willing to come out of her shell a little, in time. Meanwhile, would you like to see her?"

"Oh, I didn't know if I would be able to. Yes please, if that's okay, doctor."

"Certainly. We wouldn't usually recommend visits from relatives, as often it causes distress to the patients, but I think in this case we'll make an exception. Perhaps if she knows you are there, we may be able to get somewhere. Any information we can gauge from her will be valuable in determining our next steps."

James followed Doctor Lynch down a dull green, seemingly endless corridor, where they reached the door to Anna's room. As a courtesy, or perhaps old habits, the doctor knocked on the door prior to entering, despite Anna lying in bed in a listless state. James was shocked by what he saw. She seemed to have deteriorated even further in the space of two days. Her hair was greasy and lank, sticking to her head with clumps missing. Her jaundiced face was gaunt, her mouth drawn in from where her teeth were missing. Her cheekbones were prominent in a ghastly, skeletal manner, and her eyes sat like black hollows in their sockets, staring blindly at the bare wall opposite. She had lost half of her body weight and looked like a corpse.

"Hello, Anna. Your husband is here to see you, isn't that nice?" Doctor Lynch spoke in a gentle voice.

"Hi darling," said James, forcing himself to lean in to kiss her cheek, trying his best to ignore the rancid smell emanating from his wife. "I've been worried about you."

What happened next came as a shock to the doctor as much as James. Anna turned her head slowly to look him dead in the eye, her thin mouth curling upwards into a twisted, toothless smile.

"How's Angie?" she sneered; her breath putrid as if her mouth was harbouring something rotten. "Pretty little thing, isn't she? Young, too. Just how you like them."

James staggered back in fright as Anna reverted her gaze back to the wall, her expression languid once more.

"Who, may I ask, is Angie?" queried Doctor Lynch excitedly. "This is the most progress we have had from your wife since she arrived; she hasn't interacted at all with anybody until now!"

"I can't - I mean - I don't know…I'm sorry, I need to go!" James cried, pushing past the doctor in haste.

"Wait, please - Mr Hayward!"

James fled the hospital without a second glance back. The way Anna's eyes had seared into him with that ghastly smile tormented him. Her image burned into his head. How did she know about Angie? The more he thought about it, the more he was beginning to come to terms with the idea that something foul was at play.

14

Later that night in bed, James was restless. He tossed and turned, as he was met with the grotesque, emaciated image of Anna smiling at him whenever he closed his eyes. He had tried to dull the thoughts of her with more whiskey but that hadn't helped. Instead, he cast his mind back to her standing in the kitchen pleading with him, telling him how she had been attacked and how he hadn't believed her. He had let his temper get the better of him as always. He kept thinking about what she had said in the hospital bed about Angie and how she could have known. He was always so careful to cover his tracks; not once had she caught him, in all his years of being unfaithful. Yet, somehow, she had known about this one.

He was relieved when dawn finally broke, and watery sunlight trickled through the shutters, deciding he would phone the hospital first thing and then go into work as usual.

He picked up his phone and saw he had two missed calls and one voice message. It was from the police.

"Mr Hayward, this is Detective Inspector Chris Barnes. It's important we speak to you concerning your wife. Could you please give me a call back on this number as soon as possible."

James swallowed hard. The net was beginning to close around him. He knew what this looked like from the outside. Battered wife, sexual assault. These things never ended well for the spouse.

I can't go to fucking prison. I know what they'd do to someone like me.

He buried the thought as he dialled the number for the hospital. The police could wait.

"Good morning, Doctor Lynch's office," the receptionist answered.

"Yes, hello, good morning. James Hayward here. I'm calling for an update on my wife."

"One moment, please. I'll put you through now."

"Hello, Mr Hayward. Doctor Lynch speaking."

"Good morning, Doctor. Just phoning to see how Anna is getting on? Has there been any improvement overnight?" James asked in a feigned attempt at sounding concerned.

"I'm afraid not, Mr Hayward. I was rather hoping that, after seeing you yesterday and having that moment of lucidity, she may have shown some signs of improvement but, if anything, I'd say her condition seems to have deteriorated even further. She is refusing to eat or drink, so we've had to hook her up to a drip."

James sighed. "What can be done for her, do you think?"

"We are going to run some more tests on her today. It concerns me how she looks to have lost more weight overnight, but we are hoping the IV will help stabilise her. In terms of how she is doing mentally, I really couldn't say. We have had to sedate her, as she was ripping the tubes out and, without fluids, she really was hanging in the balance. I've never seen anything quite like this before."

"I'll do my best to get there early this evening, Doctor. I'll make my way up straight from work."

James hung up and walked into the kitchen. Anna's handbag was hanging on the back of the door. He could see an old, leather-bound book peeking out from the top and pulled it out. He sat down at the kitchen island and opened the book. It was written in strange prose with bizarre looking amulets illustrated on each page. An uncomfortable feeling crept over him and he felt the hairs on the back of neck stand on end. He knew this book was linked to what was happening to Anna in some way but couldn't think how. As he flicked through the pages, a small piece of paper fell out. On it was written a name.

Vadoma Lakatos.

Underneath it was a phone number. James picked up his mobile again and hesitated before dialling, unsure of what to say but knowing that the key to finding out what was wrong with his wife likely lay with this person.

He took a deep breath and dialled the number. It took a few moments before the phone was answered, but he was finally met with a male voice.

"Hello?"

"Hello. I'm sorry to call out of the blue, but I'm hoping you can help me please. I'm calling about my wife, Anna. Anna Hayward"

"I don't know of anyone by that name," answered the voice.

James paused. "Oh, well perhaps you can help me with something else. I'm looking for a Vadoma Lakatos."

There was a long silence. "Vadoma was my wife, and I'm afraid she can't help you with anything either."

"Why not?"

"My wife is dead, Mr Hayward. Now if that is all, then I bid you good day."

"Wait, please don't hang up - your wife, did she ever mention anyone called Anna to you?"

"Mr Hayward, I'm sorry I can't help you - I must go," argued the man on the other end of the line.

"Listen, please. Anna has a book belonging to your wife. A strange book, it's full of, well, spells or something? Please - if you know something which could help me, anything at all?"

"A book?"

"Yes, it's full of weird stuff. Creepy looking shit. But your wife's name was inside, written on a piece of paper."

"You said Anna is your wife?" asked the man, his tone changing. "Then you need to listen to me very carefully. Your wife is in grave danger. She visited Vadoma the night before she died. I am afraid she has encountered a very dangerous entity, which has attached itself to her. The book you are holding contains a spell which was intended to break the attachment. Tell me, where is your wife now?"

James explained in detail the turn of events which had happened over the last couple of days whilst the man, who had introduced himself as Jozsef, listened intently.

"So, as you can see," concluded James, "I really don't know what else to do?"

"I don't think there is anything you or I can do, Mr Hayward. It's in God's hands now. Is your wife a religious woman?"

"She is a lapsed Catholic. Her parents were killed in a car accident, many years back. Anna had to identify the bodies, both of which had been horrifically mutilated and, since then, she has struggled with her faith. I don't think she ever fully came to terms with it."

"God may be all she has left now. My advice to you would be to get in touch with the Church. Your wife may need the help of a priest before it's too late. I'm sorry I can't be of any more help, Mr Hayward," concluded the man, before hanging up.

James stood for some time, staring at the book in his hands. A priest? What good would that do, he wondered. He knew Anna's views on the Church and was struggling to come to terms with the idea that this could be, in any way, supernatural. He was an atheist. He didn't believe in God or Heaven so, by that reasoning, he couldn't bring himself to believe in the possibility of demons or Hell. It was all nonsense to him. Whatever was wrong with Anna, he was sure there had to be a medical explanation. She'd always had a morbid curiosity with death and the afterlife so, perhaps, her dabbling in this nonsense may have triggered some sort of mental breakdown; but that was the closest he was prepared to believe in its involvement.

The rest of the day dragged, and James had difficulty concentrating at work. He was on a short fuse from the lack of sleep and issues surrounding Anna, so his colleagues kept their distance. They knew him to be hot headed, at the best of times, and could read his mood from the moment he walked into the office. By four pm, he had packed up and was ready to head to Radcliffe to see Anna.

The drive felt long and arduous, and he was continually plagued with images of her from the night before. The distortion of her face, the twisted smile. He was nervous at what he might be faced with when he reached the hospital. Would she have deteriorated further? Would she even recognise him? Did he even want her to?

The building loomed ahead as he pulled into the car park. It looked every bit as solemn on the exterior as it was inside. Parts of it were dilapidated and seemed at risk of collapse. Paint was peeling from the tired walls and the small windows had bars over them. It had been used as an asylum for the criminally insane many years ago, but it seemed little had been done to reinvent it as a psychiatric hospital. It looked and felt more like a prison with all the bars and locks.

He walked in and was met with the familiar smell of bleach and antiseptic, masking an underlying odour of something far more unpleasant. Urine, faeces, blood, perhaps all three. He couldn't be sure, but it made his stomach turn, and he had to swallow hard to stop himself from retching.

Doctor Lynch was already standing in reception, talking to one of the nurses.

"Ah, good evening, Mr Hayward," he said fervently. "I trust you are well? Come, I'll take you to see Anna. We can talk as we walk."

The two men walked down the long corridor towards Anna's room, the lights above them flickering as they passed. Doctor Lynch shot a cursory glance at the ceiling.

"Old buildings, the wiring is a nightmare."

James laughed nervously, as he was beginning to question whether there really was something more sinister going on than he had first believed. There was a sense of foreboding in the air and every fibre of his being wanted to return to the comfort of his car and leave this godforsaken place.

"You'll be pleased to hear we saw some improvement today, after all. Shortly after our phone call, the duty nurse came to find me, saying she'd found Anna sitting up in bed. She'd been talking and appeared to be making some sense. She even managed to eat a little of her breakfast. It was porridge, of course, as that's all she can really manage with her mouth the way it is. She didn't know why she was here, but she did ask for you. When we told her you were coming to see her later, she seemed to perk up considerably."

"Oh really? Well, that's something then, isn't it? Have you run any more tests?" James wasn't sure why Anna's sudden improvement unnerved him somewhat, but he covered his discomfort as best he could. Something about this wasn't right at all.

"We haven't run any invasive tests just yet, as we thought that, given her responsiveness today, we'd focus on further observations. We thought perhaps this evening we could wheel her through to the communal area, where she could be amongst other patients. She might feel more at ease having you with her."

James nodded in agreement as they approached Anna's room. He wasn't sure whether his nerves were due to anxiety or shame, as Doctor Lynch opened the door, but he didn't have long to think about it.

The stench was overpowering as they entered the room, forcing both men to cover their faces. Blood and excrement were smeared on the walls, and Anna was rocking on the edge of the bed, laughing. Her hands and gown were also covered in excrement, and she raised a hand to point at James, her mouth wide open in a toothless grin. With a manic look in her eyes, she then brought her hand back to her face and, to James' horror, began licking it off her fingers.

"Aren't you going to come and kiss your wife?" she snarled.

Doctor Lynch rushed forward but, before he could tend to her, Anna stood up and pushed him with such force that he was thrown across the room and knocked out cold.

Anna padded slowly across the room to James, the grotesque grin expanding to the point where it almost consumed the width of her face, before dropping her gown to the floor, exposing her ravaged body. James backed towards the door, but it had closed behind him, so there was nowhere to go. He turned and pulled frantically at the handle, but the door was jammed.

"Don't act so afraid, darling," she leered. "I'm not going to hurt you. I just want things to be better between us, like they used to be." She stopped inches from his face, her eyes like dark pools and her mouth, a black, empty crater where her teeth had once been. Her breath was foul as she reached out and grabbed his cock, squeezing it hard.

"Why don't I show you how much I've missed you, James." She reached for his belt and pulled it off in one swift movement. Tugging at his jeans, she knelt in front of him. He tried to resist, but she was too strong and the way her hands got to work on his cock quickly brought him to a semi state of disgusted arousal. He closed his eyes, so he didn't have to look at her, but let out a sigh in twisted delight as she slid her lips around him, drawing him deeply into her damp crater of a mouth. She had never sucked his cock so fervently before, yet here she was, taking the full length and girth of him with ease. With no teeth in the way, his cock slid inside her warm, wet mouth with ease, and as much as he hated to admit, it felt good.

Just as he was about to relieve himself into her gaping mouth, she clamped her jaw around him hard. James cried out as he pulled himself out of her, looking down in anger and fear, repulsed by what he saw.

"Get the fuck away from me, you lunatic! You disgust me."

Darkness washed over Anna's face, her smile turning to a sneer.

"You'll be sorry for what you did to me. He'll see that you pay. All those women you abused. You think you hold all the power, but you have nothing. He'll drive you to insanity, soon you'll be begging him for mercy, pleading for death as you relive your worst nightmares. All of your ghosts will come back to haunt you, just you wait and see!"

She made a lunge at James just as the door burst open, and another doctor, accompanied by two male nurses, entered.

"What in God's name has gone on here?" roared the doctor, scanning the room. He immediately rushed over to Doctor Lynch, who was coming round and cradling his head, moaning. One of the nurses tended to Anna who, as if on cue, had slipped back into delirium and was rocking on the floor. James pulled his jeans up in haste and tried to explain what had happened.

"It's not how it looks," he pleaded. "She hurled Doctor Lynch across the room before attacking me!"

"We'll see whether that is the case when we check the CCTV," scolded the doctor. "Now, if you don't mind, I think it's best you leave while we take control of this."

James left the hospital distraught. Bleak thoughts filled his head on the drive home, where the half full whiskey bottle from the night before sat waiting, ready to be finished.

15

Anna woke at around two am that night. The room was dark and silent. Moments of lucidity were rare and mostly seemed to be when nobody else was around. Her body was battered and bruised, and every fibre of her being ached. She tried lifting her arm, but it was a dead weight. It was as if she was no longer in control of her own body, and her mind was trapped inside a vessel which no longer belonged to her.

She heard the echo of slow footsteps outside in the corridor, pausing when they reached her door which then creaked open slowly. She turned her head towards it with difficulty to see a dark figure standing in the doorway.

"Can you feel me inside of you, Anna?" teased the voice from the shadows. "We had fun with him today, didn't we?"

Anna tried to open her mouth, but no words would come out.

"No need to speak, I'm already inside your head. My control over you is growing stronger by the day, you are making it rather easy for me," the voice laughed softly.

The figure stepped forward, reaching inside his suit jacket for a cigarette. The warm glow of the match lit up his face, enabling Anna to see him clearly. He was a man again, not a monster, and he looked even more handsome than she remembered. He smiled as he approached the bed, tracing a hand tenderly down her body.

"I'm sorry about your teeth," he said. "But it's not like you'll be needing those now, and I think even your husband would agree the important things feel so much better without those getting in the way. However, this..." he added, resting his hand between her legs, "is something I very much still have a use for."

He slid his hand under her gown and gently prised her legs apart, her body weightless under his touch as she responded by grinding herself against him. She moaned softly as his fingers slipped inside her, hooking her towards him as he bent down and licked her wet folds.

"You belong to me, Anna," he growled. "Every part of you is mine."

He lapped at her with insatiable intent, and she gripped his head between her thighs, her back arching as waves of pleasure consumed her. When he eventually emerged from under her gown, he leaned in to kiss her, and she could taste her own juices on his tongue as she whimpered in delight.

"Fuck me," she pleaded.

"I'm inside you already, Anna. All you have to do is close your eyes and imagine."

He ran his fingers lightly over her eyes to shut them and retreated from the room as Anna fell into a sound sleep. She felt herself being pulled in different directions, her breasts being groped by unseen hands and warm, wet tongues lapping hungrily at her cunt. She was losing herself within a playground of pleasure and pain, gradually sacrificing her body over to it. An unseen phallus probed her from behind, forcing its way deep inside her anal passage. She had never experienced this before and the double penetration awakened new, unfulfilled urges.

As she felt herself close to climax she saw the true face of the demon once more. His hideous grin stretched across his face, his bloated belly harbouring the vile mouth which snarled at Anna ravenously; what looked to be distorted faces and hands pressed up inside the creature's stomach, wailing and trying to make their way out. The souls of the damned.

She realised then that Hell was not only a place, but also a state of mind – both of which she would soon have no control over.

16

It was close to midday when James woke to the sound of police sirens, which had him jolt up in a panic. Were they coming for him? He felt sick to the stomach as he froze in panic, not knowing whether to stay put or make a run for it. The sirens came closer before fading and he exhaled a sigh of relief, as he realised they had passed by the house. He got out of bed, squinting at the sunlight coming through the window. It had been a restless night, full of dreams of endless corridors and liminal space where, no matter how far he ran, he was unable to find his way out. He had sensed something behind, creeping up on him, but whenever he turned, there was nothing there. As he crossed the corridor over to the bathroom, he couldn't bring himself to look down the dim passageway towards the master bedroom, where he had found Anna.

The house felt eerily still, yet he could sense an energy: dark, heavy, and foreboding. He hadn't experienced it before, and it caused a shiver to run down his spine. He thought back to all the times he had ridiculed Anna before when she had spoken of it.

After a shower, he made coffee and turned on the television. He sat for some time, just working his way through the channels, desperate to take his mind off his unravelling life.

With a sigh, he turned the television off, but as the screen turned black, he jumped upon seeing what looked to be the reflection of a man standing behind him in the doorway. Startled, he turned but there was nobody there. When he looked back at the television screen, the doorway was empty.

I'm losing my mind.

Unable to shift the growing unease, he recalled the conversation he'd had with Jozsef on the phone. Perhaps speaking to a priest wouldn't be such a bad idea, given the latest turn of events. Anna didn't seem to be getting any better; in fact, she was getting worse. Perhaps they might be able to cast some light on the matter where the doctors couldn't.

He picked up his phone and searched for local Catholic churches. Before he was even certain of what to say, he had dialled the number of the first one he found local to him.

He was greeted on the other end of the line by a lady with a friendly voice.

"Oh, yes. Good morning. I'm not even sure why I'm phoning, but I think I need to speak with a priest. It's about my wife, she's very sick."

"Oh dear, I'm very sorry to hear that," said the lady. "Is your wife a member of our church?"

"No, she hasn't been to church for a very long time, but she's not of sound mind and has been sectioned. We can't get to the bottom of what is wrong with her though, and I spoke with someone who thinks she might have some sort of attachment."

"An attachment?" the lady asked. "What do you mean?"

"A spirit attachment."

There was silence for a few moments as James heard her place the phone down and walk away. He could hear muffled voices talking in the background.

"I see," she said, returning to the phone. "Well, in that case, you need to meet with Father Byrne. He isn't at this church; he is a little further away at our sister church in Bermondsey. One moment please, let me fetch his details."

She returned a few moments later with the information about the other church. James thanked her and hung up.

He stared at the details, written on a scrap of paper in his hand. It was time to go pay this Father Byrne a visit. If all this could be pinned on a possible spirit attachment, it could be the very thing to take the heat off him.

17

James took the tube to Bermondsey the following morning. South London wasn't a place he was overly familiar with, and he always felt ill at ease travelling to places out of his sphere of influence. As he resurfaced to street level, he looked around. Bermondsey was everything he had expected it to be: grey, bleak, and overcrowded. Cursing pedestrians pushed past him as he stood on the pavement gaining his bearings. Pulling his phone from his jacket pocket, he brought up the details of Father Byrne's church and started to walk. It was raining, and he could feel a chill in the air, although he didn't know how much of that could be attributed to his mounting trepidation at what lay ahead.

Before long, he saw the church up ahead. It was a magnificent building, grand in stature, and loomed imposingly over the grey post-war architecture surrounding it. Enormous, intricately designed stained glass windows adorned the church. It looked like an oasis of calm within a concrete jungle.

Since stepping off the tube, he couldn't shake the feeling that he was being followed. He glanced over his shoulder a few times and caught sight of a well-dressed gentleman in a suit, who appeared to be watching him but vanished in the crowd as quickly as he was spotted. As he walked through the cemetery towards the church entrance, he felt uneasy and picked up his pace, almost breaking into a run by the time he reached the main door. He hated cemeteries at the best of times, but today felt worse than usual.

The door creaked open, and he stepped inside the building. The cool air hit him, and he was filled with a sense of peace as he closed the door behind him, leaving his fears at its threshold.

Up ahead, he noticed an elderly lady tending to an array of flowers adorning the altar.

"Excuse me," he said. "I'm looking for Father Byrne."

She turned and met him with a smile. "He's just in his office, is he expecting you?"

"No, umm…sorry, I should have called ahead. I was advised to get in touch with him through my local church. It's a very sensitive matter, you see. They thought he might be able to help."

"One moment, I'll go see if he is free." The lady shuffled off, disappearing through a door leading to the back of the church.

After a few minutes, she emerged followed out by a stoic looking priest who introduced himself as Father Byrne. He looked to be in his seventies, with eyes belonging to someone who had witnessed the world and all the darkness within it.

"Good morning, how can I help you?" Father Byrne spoke with a soft Irish accent and extended a hand to James, meeting him with a firmer grip than James had anticipated. This was a strong man, not to be messed with.

"Morning, Father. My name is James Hayward. I realise I probably should have called ahead to let you know I was coming, but I feel this is a conversation I needed to have face to face with you, and I'm not even sure where to start."

Before James could say any more, Father Byrne nodded and gestured for him to follow him towards another door. Ushering him through it, he led James to his office. The room was aged with the musky aroma associated with a clergy room, as if it had not been aired in some time. Rows of books lined the walls, some of which looked so old they would be at risk of falling apart when opened. The priest sat down behind a heavy oak desk, piles of books and paperwork scattered across it, and pointed to the brown leather chair opposite for James to sit.

"It's okay, I think I have an idea why you are here. I received a call yesterday afternoon from our sister church up in Hampstead, telling me I could expect a visit. I understand it's to do with a spiritual attachment?"

Relieved at the priest already knowing the reason for him being there, James proceeded to tell him everything that had happened to date, starting with the scratches Anna insisted she had heard in the walls, to where she currently was in the psychiatric hospital.

Father Byrne listened intently, his brow weighted by a heavy frown as his dark eyes studied James, nodding in appropriate places without interruption. He remained solemn, his hands clasped together in careful consideration as James explained Anna's rapidly deteriorating condition, including the details about what had happened when he had last visited.

After he had finished speaking, they sat in silence for several moments before the priest cleared his throat and spoke.

"I believe you, Mr Hayward," he said in a reassuring manner. "As much as I wish it weren't true, it does sound as though your wife is exhibiting symptoms of possession. Of course, I would need to see her for myself to be certain. Tell me, where exactly is your wife being treated?"

"Radcliffe House. It's just north of..."

"I know the place," Father Byrne interrupted. "From what you have told me, she seems to be deteriorating at great speed so, if we are to have any chance of saving her, we have little time to spare. I suggest we visit her this evening."

"So, there is a chance of saving her then, Father?" James asked, nervously.

"It depends how much of her is left," the priest replied. "Physically, it may be too late but there is still a chance we can save her soul from eternal damnation."

James felt his mouth go dry and swallowed hard. This was all too real. Up until now, the prospect of facing up to the possibility of a demonic attachment had been nothing more than a last resort, buried safely away at the back of his mind. He had been willing to let the doctors treat it as psychosis and run their array of medical tests on Anna. On sharing her story, he had half expected, or hoped, the priest would have dismissed it as nonsense, but instead it was quite the opposite. Father Byrne hadn't hesitated to confirm his worst fears.

"I am going to need a little time to pray and prepare for this, Mr Hayward. If indeed I confirm the worst, upon meeting with Anna, I must warn you we may need to prepare for an exorcism. I don't know how much you know about these, but it's important that you realise the risks involved. First of all, I would require permission from the Church, as this is not something which can be undertaken lightly, nor can I perform it alone. I would need to draw upon others to assist me, and it is no easy task. Not many are prepared to do this, and there are only a small handful of us in this country who are equipped to do so. This is why it is so important that I meet with your wife as soon as possible, so we know for sure what it is we are dealing with."

"I understand enough from what I've seen in films," answered James.

"A real exorcism is nothing like what you may have seen in the movies, Mr Hayward. It is not a case of simply throwing around some holy water and words from the Bible; it takes a serious toll on the mind and body of anyone involved. There is a very real threat to the life of anyone who partakes in it, not least the person being exorcised. Often, an exorcism can only serve to make matters worse."

"I can't see how things could possibly get any worse," muttered James.

"You'd be surprised, Mr Hayward. Meet me back here at four pm and we can travel there together."

18

Father Byrne saw James to the door and closed it behind him softly. He retired to his desk and exhaled deeply, resting his head in his hands. He sat for a few moments focusing on his breathing and trying to quell the uneasy feeling in his stomach. The serpent inside, which had lain dormant for all these years, was stirring. He had felt it in his morning prayers. He knew this day would eventually come, whether he was ready for it or not.

He reached inside the bottom drawer and pulled out a bottle of Scotch. He opened it and the smell turned his stomach, but he still took a long, hard mouthful. He had sworn he wouldn't drink another drop of this poison, but it wasn't every day you had to pay the Devil himself a visit, and many decades had passed since they were last acquainted.

The priest winced as the liquor hit the back of his throat, the warm liquid seeping down as it got to work. The anxiety, nestled deep within the confines of his mind, had unravelled at the prospect of what lay ahead. He knew what he had to do. There was only one person he could confide in and relay his worst fears.

With trembling hands, he reached back inside the drawer and pulled out a small black book. He flicked through the pages until he found the contact he was looking for. It was a Croatian number, scribbled lightly in pencil, which had faded on the page over time, but he could still make out the numbers faintly. He just hoped the number still belonged to the person he needed.

He dialled it, and there was a long pause before a voice answered on the other end of the line.

Father Byrne took a deep breath and swallowed hard.

"It's back."

19

James stepped out of the church, breathed deeply, and lifted his head to the sky, letting the rain wash over him. As he straightened up and started to walk, he caught sight of a smartly dressed man moving ahead of him between the headstones. It looked to be the same man he had seen earlier, who had followed him from the station.

"Hey!" James shouted. "Wait!"

The man turned towards James and smiled darkly, before disappearing behind a cluster of large tombstones concealed within the trees on the perimeter of the graveyard. James hurried down the path to catch up with him.

By the time he had reached the perimeter, there was no sign of the man anywhere. As far as James could see, there was only one way in and out of the churchyard, so he could not understand how he had seemingly vanished into thin air.

An uneasy feeling came over him and, despite not being able to see the man, he couldn't shake the feeling of being watched.

James made his way back to the main street and hurried towards the tube. He had several hours to kill before reconvening with Father Byrne and was glad to be leaving the streets of Bermondsey behind.

He didn't feel like going home, telling himself that he just needed to be around other people, and it had nothing to do with not wanting to be alone in the house.

Disembarking at Hampstead, he decided to go to his local pub, opting to sit on his own at a table at the back. He wanted to be in the presence of others, yet alone with his thoughts. Picking up his phone and scrolling, he quickly realised that searching for stories on exorcisms was a mistake. Some of the images he found were horrific, suddenly realising how gruelling a process this was. He had selfishly hoped that, if this was something Anna would be faced with, he wouldn't need to be involved in any way. He wondered just what sort of a wife he would be left with if the exorcism was a success. Would she return to the way she had been, or would he be left with a shell of the woman she once was, nothing but a living corpse? And how could they be sure whatever this was wouldn't come back? Endless questions filled his head, and he wasn't even sure if he wanted Anna back. He slammed the phone down on the table and stared into his empty pint glass, oblivious to the smartly dressed man watching him from a dark corner of the bar.

The afternoon passed slowly, and James found himself wandering the streets aimlessly as he killed time. When four pm eventually came, he made the journey south again to meet Father Byrne at the church.

The priest was waiting for him outside by the time James arrived. He seemed nervous and kept looking over his shoulder as they walked to his car, as if he had been spooked by something but assured James that he was fine.

When they were safely in the car, the priest turned to James.

"Listen, Mr Hayward. I need to be honest with you about something. If it turns out that your wife is in need of an exorcism, I'm not sure I can be the one to do it. You see, I attempted one many years ago and…" his voice trailed off as his eyes clouded over, looking into the distance.

"What happened?" James asked.

The priest sighed. "I failed her."

"Failed her? What do you mean?"

"She died, Mr Hayward."

The two men sat in silence, looking ahead as the rain drummed down against the window.

"And you think that might happen again with my wife?" James asked after a long pause.

"If this is the same entity we are dealing with, and I am certain it is, I cannot guarantee the safety of your wife. This is a powerful demon, and it is no accident you came to me. For he is a master of his craft and has woven a web that has us both entwined. I met him once, many years ago, and as I looked in his eyes, I knew we would meet again. That much he told me. I pray I am wrong, and that your wife is not in his grasp, but if my fears are correct, we are going to need help from elsewhere."

"Who else can help us, Father? I came to you because I was told you were the only one who could help."

"Ordinary spirit attachments, yes, those are easy to banish providing you have the faith. Low level astral beings are no match against the power of Christ. But this is not any ordinary attachment. This entity mirrors the Devil himself, and I am an old man. I am no match for that. I made a call earlier this afternoon to an old colleague I worked with years ago on a mission in Europe. He is an expert on demonology and may be able to help us. The only problem we have now,

Mr Haywood, is time. We may not have much of that on our side."

They made the rest of the journey to Radcliffe in silence, an oppressive atmosphere in the car. Both men knew the significance of the journey and neither wished to speak of what might be lying ahead. Father Byrne kept his eyes fixed firmly on the road, his hands gripping the wheel so tightly that his knuckles turned white.

James' stomach sank as he saw the ominous psychiatric hospital looming ahead. It was starting to get dark, which gave the whole place an even more sinister appearance, and he could feel his heart beating in his throat. Father Byrne gave nothing away in his expression, appearing lost in his thoughts.

As they entered the hospital, James was hit with the familiar smell of antiseptic and bleach, attempting to mask whatever obnoxious undertone was in the air. He raised a sleeve to his hand, in a vain attempt to stifle it, but the priest seemed unfazed. It was as if this underlying odour was no stranger to him.

Walking over to the reception desk, James rang the bell. Moments later, the receptionist appeared.

"Yes?" she asked wearily.

"I'd like to speak with someone concerning my wife please. She is a resident here. Anna Hayward."

The receptionist glared at James from over the top of her glasses.

"You were here to see Doctor Lynch the other day, weren't you? He's in the hospital himself now, no thanks to your wife. I'll have to see who else is available."

With a sigh, she picked up the phone and dialled through to the medical team before nodding vaguely over to the seating area, gesturing for the two men to wait.

"Someone will be with you shortly," she said, placing the handset down.

A few minutes later, they were greeted by a young doctor who introduced herself as Doctor Kashani.

"Mr Hayward?" She extended a hand to James. "And I'm sorry, I didn't catch your name?" she added, offering her hand to Father Byrne.

"This is my wife's priest," James said quickly, before the older man had a chance to speak. "We thought she might benefit from a visit."

"Oh, well, yes of course. She isn't in any fit state to recognise anyone, but I can't see what harm it could do. Come this way, I'll take you to her. I'm afraid you'll need to prepare yourselves as her appearance may come as a shock."

Doctor Kashani turned on her heel and led the way as James and the priest exchanged an apprehensive look at what lay in wait.

James took a deep breath as the doctor turned the key in the door.

"I have to ask, Doctor. Is my wife being locked up for her own protection or for the protection of others?"

The doctor paused without looking up.

"For both reasons, Mr Hayward," she answered as the door swung open. "I shall wait outside and let you have a few minutes alone with her."

James gasped as he entered the room and saw Anna lying in bed. Her wrists and ankles were badly bruised from where they had been shackled to the bed. She looked emaciated. Her eyes were sunken craters, and her cracked lips were drawn against blackened, bare gums. She writhed in pain and seemed oblivious to the two men who had entered the room. It was only when Father Byrne stepped forward that she froze, before turning her head towards him in a feigned, coquettish manner.

"Hello Father, we meet again." A scornful voice emerged from deep within Anna as she broke into a twisted grin. Her eyes burned into the priest, and he took a step forward.

"With whom do I speak?" Father Byrne asked, the tremor in his voice detectable.

Anna threw her head back, her spine twisting in a grotesque manner. "I go by the names of many. But you know me as one." She smiled perversely.

"Tell me," asked the priest, stepping forward.

"B.E.L.I.A.L," Anna answered, expelling each letter from her mouth like venom.

Father Byrne gasped and edged backwards, reaching for the chair to steady himself. James felt an inexplicable chill pass through him, and a heaviness settle on his shoulders.

"No, it can't be," he exclaimed. "You took the soul of that young girl before I banished you back to the depths of Hell where you belong. Why have you come back? What do you want from this woman?"

"This whore is of no concern to me. She is merely a vessel for me to feed from. I have unfinished business here. Earth has too many temptations, but you know that for yourself, don't you, Father?"

A glimmer of shame crept across the priest's face as he turned to face James, guiding him back towards the door, while Anna flailed and cackled wildly on the bed.

"This confirms my suspicions, Mr Hayward, but it's much worse than I thought. The entity attached to your wife is a powerful one, and he has taken so much of her already. I'm not sure how much of her remains to be saved, but I do know I am no match for him alone. We must leave now so I can make the necessary calls."

20

Anna heard the door open, and it took every ounce of energy she had to turn and face it. Inside, she was screaming for James to hear her pleas, but they went unanswered. He looked at her with such disdain, accompanied by a priest which she knew could only mean one of two things. Either she was close to death, and he was here to read her Last Rites, of which she would beg to be free of this suffering, or he was here to help banish this entity eating away at her. She could feel her strength waning by the hour; she knew she didn't have much time left on this earth physically but feared for her soul. For, if she died with this entity attached, what would happen to her? Her body might be free of it, but her soul would be imprisoned for eternity. Each time she tried to pray, it heard her and blocked her thoughts, sending a piercing pain to her very core.

When the priest approached her, and she had opened her mouth to speak, it was not her voice emanating from her body but that of the demon.

Belial.

Lord Of Lies. Master of Deception.

He was the master, and she was the puppet. Her body was nothing more than a cesspit harbouring evil. She knew now how foolish she had been submitting to him, for he did not care for her. She was nothing more than a conduit for his demons to feed from. There were many of them in there with her, clutching at her, fighting over her body like starved wolves.

She just wanted it to end and no longer cared if this meant death. Her life, as she knew it, was already over so what did she have left to live for? Her body was in a state of ruin, her mind close to being lost, and she had nothing to fight for any longer. Even God had abandoned her, just like he had abandoned her all those years ago when he took her parents away so cruelly. If there was a God, to what lengths would one need to suffer in order for him to hear? Her parents had both been God-fearing Catholics, who went to church each Sunday and tried their best to live good Christian lives only to end up dying a slow, agonising death, when their car was dragged under the wheels of a passing lorry. Now here she lay, helpless at the mercy of Lucifer himself, whilst God was nowhere to be seen.

When James and the priest had entered the room, she had seen him standing behind them. Sneering coldly as he pulled her strings, her arms and legs no longer belonging to her as they thrashed on the bed, her spine contorted to the point that she felt it might break. She begged him to stop, but he continued, mocking her cruelly as he watched her writhe on the bed. His words flowed from her mouth, making her choke, cold eyes watching her as he orchestrated every movement, whilst the men remained blind to his presence.

She saw him approach the priest as he spoke and watched him lean into the old man's face closely, teeth bared, snarling the words which came out of Anna's mouth before turning to her and smiling. She knew neither man would be able to fight him for his strength was centuries old, drawing on all the forces from the depths of Hell itself. But the way he had looked at James longingly, despite everything Belial had done to her, she couldn't help but feel a pang of jealousy. He had moved from the priest to stand behind James, placing his hands on his shoulders and breathing him in. It was as if they had a shared purpose. Had he got into James' head too?

Anna knew then that she was bound to Belial for all eternity, and there would be nothing the man of God could do about it.

21

Upon leaving the room, and hearing Anna's manic howling echoing down the corridor, the two men sought out Doctor Kashani, who had been called over to assist with another patient who had broken free from her restraints and was lashing out in a fit of rage as two nurses wrestled her to the floor.

"I'm sorry for abandoning you, gentlemen," said the doctor as she scrambled to her feet, having administered the hysterical patient with a sedative. "So many of our residents seem out of sorts, even more than usual at the moment. We've got our hands full with them. They all seem restless, it's as if a fox has been let loose amongst the chickens."

"You may very well be right about that," said Father Byrne, under his breath. "Would you mind if I took a look over Mrs Hayward's medical records? There's something I would like to discuss with you in private please, if you don't mind."

"We wouldn't usually share –"

"Doctor," interrupted Father Byrne. "With all due respect, there is nothing usual about this case."

Upon entering Radcliffe, the priest could sense the presence of the demon. The smell which accompanied him was rife in the air and one that he had experienced before. As they had walked through the ward, he had noticed how the presence had made itself felt amongst the other residents; there was a bubbling undercurrent of unsettled behaviour. The priest knew it wasn't unusual for those experiencing psychological illness to be more in tune with the spirit world, as mental boundaries put in place to condition the human brain into not believing in such beings were inadvertently lifted.

Doctor Kashani led the men into her office and closed the door softly behind her.

"I'll be honest with you, Doctor, and cut to the chase," said Father Byrne. "I don't believe for one minute Anna Hayward is suffering from a psychiatric disorder. I believe she is, in fact, suffering from a demonic attachment."

James braced himself for a condescending reaction from the doctor but, conversely, she fixed her gaze on them and nodded slowly in agreement.

"I'm listening," she said. "The scientist in me wants to disagree with you, but all the evidence seems to point to the contrary. I've dedicated my career to this field and never once have I ever come across anything like this before. None of the tests we have carried out indicate there is anything clinically wrong with Anna, yet her physical demise and waning lucidity concerns us. Quite frankly, my colleagues and I are at a loss as to what we can try next. What is it you are suggesting we do, Father?"

"If I'm being honest, what Anna needs is an exorcism," said Father Byrne bluntly.

The doctor cradled her head in her hands as she sighed. "They'd never allow that here. There has to be another way to help her."

"With all due respect, this is the only option open to us now. We've surpassed everything else. If we don't act soon, Anna will die," said the priest.

"If we are to do this, then it can't be here. If the authorities found out about this, we could be shut down, and I could never practise medicine again."

"We should do it at the house, it's where all of this started after all. Whatever this is that has a hold over my wife is also connected to our house," said James. He had been silent until this point, coming to terms with the new reality that he was facing. For as long as he could remember, he had felt like the one who held all the power, using his bullying nature to belittle others for his own gain. Now, for the first time in his life, he felt small and powerless, not knowing how to process this.

The priest nodded in agreement. "Yes, it makes sense to do it there. Doctor, can it be arranged for Anna to return home?"

"Yes, under the circumstances I believe so. In theory, Anna is a dying woman who doesn't have much time left. She is physically too weak to pose a threat to anyone else around her now, so I could put a case forward that her final wish is to spend her last days at home. We are a psychiatric hospital after all, not a hospice."

"How soon can this be arranged?" asked Father Byrne.

"I can make the necessary arrangements immediately. Let me speak with my superior and arrange for her to be discharged, making a case for palliative care being offered at home to make her remaining time more comfortable."

The two men left the hospital. The drive back to London was arduous, and James fought the desire to close his eyes and sleep for fear of the dreams which haunted him.

"What did the demon mean when it said about unfinished business? What happened before, Father?"

"He won't stop. Your wife won't be enough for him. He will keep on destroying lives, he feeds off it. Thrives off the misery of others."

"The demon said something else to you, what did it mean about temptations? Is there something else you aren't telling me?"

The priest gripped the steering wheel tightly, eyes fixed straight ahead. "He is a liar. Don't take heed of his words. He will say anything to find your weakness. Once he finds that soft spot, it becomes easier for him to gain access to you. My advice is don't give him anything. The less we know about each other's weaknesses the better, as we can't afford to create any divisions between us, while we work together on saving your wife. We need to put up a united front. I won't poke at the skeletons in your closet Mr Hayward, and I'd appreciate you extending me the same courtesy."

They made the rest of the journey in silence. Father Byrne accompanied James to the house, saying he would need some time alone to prepare before Anna's arrival the following morning.

Upon entering the house, James felt the familiar chill run through him as he stood at the foot of the staircase and looked up into the dark void. Flicking the light switch, it came as little surprise to find the bulb had blown despite only changing it recently. He could sense eyes on him, from deep within the darkness, and the energy of the house felt stale and imposing.

"I'd like to see Anna's bedroom, please," said the priest, approaching James from behind so softly it made him jump out of his skin.

"Jesus, you nearly gave me a heart attack," yelled James, "I'd appreciate it if you didn't creep up on me like that."

"Apologies. Now, if you wouldn't mind, we don't have much time."

Father Byrne reached for the same light switch, and the hallway was illuminated.

"Wait, that wasn't working a second ago," James said.

"I'm sure this isn't the strangest thing you have witnessed here, Mr Hayward," said the priest before making his way up the stairs. "You'll need your wits about you with this entity; he has eyes everywhere and he likes to play tricks."

James swallowed hard before following the priest up the stairs, gripping the bannister tightly to disguise his hand from shaking with fear. He could feel the hairs on the back of his neck stand on end as he approached the room where Anna had been sleeping. Memories of her, crouched in the corner smeared in blood and surrounded by her own teeth, flooded his head, and he had to steady himself on the wall before opening the door. He recalled the crazed look in her eyes and shuddered.

A cold breeze swept over them as the door opened. He looked at the window, expecting it to have been left open, yet it remained tightly shut. The air was stale with a repugnant undertone, and traces of blood were evident on the floor where James had attempted to clean it. The room felt heavy, burdened with the events of what had happened within its four walls. James wondered if houses held onto memories and cast his mind back to the estate agent, who had glossed over the circumstances of death concerning the previous owner. He couldn't help but wonder if it was connected in some way to Anna, and if there was any way to find out. When he had probed the agent for more information, he had been shut down quickly and assured that the death had not happened in the property; but the surviving owner had wanted a clean break and had left the country.

Father Byrne stood in the centre of the room and closed his eyes. He took a deep breath, seemingly oblivious to the foul odour in the room, which seemed to emanate from the walls around them and was getting stronger by the minute.

"We aren't alone here, Mr Hayward," he said. "He's watching us."

"If he's here watching us, then what about Anna? What is happening to her?"

"The Devil has eyes in more than one place. Just like God. Your wife's fate hangs in the balance, and we are going to need God's assistance if we have any hope of defeating the evil that lurks in this house."

"If there is a God, then why is he letting this happen to my wife? Why can't he just stop it?"

The priest opened his eyes and turned to face James.

"Now isn't the time to be questioning the actions of God. He moves in mysterious ways just like the Devil. We have free will and your wife, I'm afraid, may have exercised hers to bring this upon herself."

James felt the rage rise inside him.

"You mean to tell me Anna did this to herself? What could she possibly have done to deserve this?"

"She invited him in," said the priest, solemnly.

The two men stood facing each other, the energy around them growing ever more tense.

"None of that matters now, though. The fact is, your wife will die without an exorcism, so we must do all we can to prepare," said Father Byrne.

22

Sleep evaded James that night, as he lay awake on the sofa, taking small comfort in the warm liquor he poured down his throat in an attempt to dull the reality of what he was facing. He watched as the watery sun rays trickled through the window. The house felt perpetually oppressive but more so at night, and he welcomed the comfort which accompanied the morning light.

Father Byrne retired early in an attempt to gather what strength he had in readiness for the next day but was met with disturbing dreams. He was back in the bedroom of the young girl in Grožnjan, except this time she was gazing up at him from the bed, beckoning him to join her.

"Won't you come here, Father?" she cooed invitingly as she opened her legs and started to touch herself.

He knew what he was doing was wrong as he removed his clothes and joined her on the bed but was unable to stop himself as the voice inside pleaded with him to stop. She was only fifteen. Every fibre of his body knew this was wrong. It was as if he was no longer in control of his body as he entered the girl. As he thrust himself inside her, he recoiled in terror as the girl's face and body contorted into that of a monstrous beast. He tried to tear himself away from the beast's clutches, but its grip was too strong as it wrestled with him, howling in delight.

"Fuck me, priest!" it bellowed.

He woke with a fright, sitting up in bed as beads of sweat rolled off him onto the soaked sheets. He jumped as the bedroom door, which he had left ajar, slammed shut with a loud bang, and he could still hear the manic laughter of the beast ringing in his ears, as if echoing down the hallway. He looked down at himself and realised in horror he was naked from the waist down and visibly aroused.

Unsure whether what he had experienced had been a dream or reality, he spent the rest of the night suspended in prayer. He hadn't planned on facing the entity alone, but there was no time to bring others in, nor did he want to for fear of things unravelling further. He had made numerous attempts to contact the Croatian priest from Grožnjan to seek advice about this demon but to no avail. Since his phone call the previous day, his subsequent messages had gone unanswered. He would need to work alone. He did not know the circumstances of why help was being refused but accepted it as his penance. This was God's will, and it was down to him, and him alone, to defeat Belial.

There had been things said to him in the hospital, which he had kept buried for years and didn't want exposed. The net surrounding him was drawing in as his secret was close to being exposed. From the little he knew of James, he didn't trust him to harbour his secret, and who knew what the entity would throw at him in order to weaken their combined effort to save Anna. He wasn't proud of his past, but he had been a different man then. Upon giving up alcohol, he considered himself a reformed man, as it hadn't just been the drink he had abused; but with Belial rearing his ugly head, he had turned back to the bottle. He was plagued with the images from his past, every time he closed his eyes, and the entity knew this was his weakness. He had battled many demons of his own and knew what he had done was unforgivable. He would never be able to forgive himself so would never expect a pardon from others either.

Daylight seemed like a blessing as he felt the warmth of the sun against his face. He shook off the intrusive thoughts that this could be his last morning on earth and focused his mind on what lay ahead.

Shortly after ten am, a private ambulance pulled up outside. Two medics, accompanied by Doctor Kashani, wheeled Anna on a stretcher into the house. James saw a wild look of panic in her eyes as she crossed the threshold, and her knuckles turned white as she gripped the sides of the stretcher in fear.

"I think it's best we take her straight upstairs, where she will be most comfortable," said Father Byrne. "Follow me," he instructed the medics.

The two men carried her up to the bedroom. Upon opening the door, they almost dropped the stretcher as they instinctively raised their hand to their faces to mask the disgusting odour. The room smelled rotten, as if someone, or something, had died in it.

"You'll have to excuse the smell, the owners have had an infestation, but it's being dealt with," said the priest.

James looked on helplessly. He was beginning to think it may have been a mistake, bringing Anna home. They were no match against this, whatever 'this' was. Father Byrne had insisted on being the one to deal with Anna's return, liaising with the medics to ensure she was provided with whatever she needed, and he felt redundant as he watched them set up the various monitors and other pieces of medical equipment. He knew all of this was futile, as there was no medical reason behind Anna's condition, but Doctor Kashani had stressed they must go along with it in order to expedite Anna's return home. James was also concerned about just how calmly the priest was dealing with this, especially given his revelation at how his last exorcism had failed and the girl had died. There was a dark history to the priest, but when James had run his name through various search engines the previous night, he could find nothing about him anywhere. It was as if Father Byrne did not exist. Perhaps the priest was right, and he shouldn't go poking around at skeletons in closets that were best left locked. James had enough of his own secrets after all. Ones which had very nearly come to the surface thanks to Anna in her delirious state.

  Later that morning, when Anna was settled in her room upstairs and the medics had departed, the two men sat down in the kitchen with Doctor Kashani to discuss what would happen next.

  Father Byrne, who had already helped himself to whiskey from one of the numerous bottles around the house, took the lead, insisting that they wait for nightfall before performing the exorcism, for that was when activity in the house was at its most prevalent.

"Now, I need you to both listen to me carefully for what we are about to undergo takes its toll enormously, both on the body and mind. Neither of you must speak with it at all for, the minute you do, it will ensnare you in its web of deceit. It feeds off your weakness and will seek to taunt and humiliate you in an attempt to break you. It will use lies to try and make us turn on each other so we lose our collective strength. This is a very dangerous entity and has the ability to disguise itself as anyone it likes, so remember that."

Doctor Kashani looked visibly shaken as she clasped her mug of tea to her chest. "Can it hurt us, Father?"

The priest took a sip of his drink and paused to light a cigarette. James cleared his throat in disapproval at the priest taking such liberties in his house but resisted the urge to say anything, as he already had more pressing doubts about the older man that were playing on his mind.

"It can only inhabit one body at a time so, unless we invite it, we are not at any risk. The danger is if Anna's body fails during the exorcism and the entity is left without a living host. This is the situation we need to avoid, and this is why it is so important you are here. Your role throughout this is to keep her alive, at any cost."

"What about me?" James asked. "What am I needed for?"

"You," replied the priest. "You are the bait, for it seems most active in your presence."

The three sat in silence for some time, each lost in their own thoughts. The silence was broken by bouts of moaning and howling from the room above, where Anna lay. None could tell whether the sounds came from Anna or the entity.

"What will the exorcism involve, exactly?" asked James.

"The aim is to drive out the demon from your wife. Under normal circumstances, if indeed there is ever such a thing as normal circumstances, we would have received a sanction from the Church that an exorcism was needed, further to a medical assessment, but given the severity of your wife's condition, we have not had the time to wait for official approval to carry this out. The ritual itself will consist of a series of prayers, statements, and appeals. The first step will be to implore the entity to vacate the body of Anna, the host, using the power of the Holy Spirit. Holy Water will be sprinkled on Anna, along with each of us in the room for our own protection. I will then recite the prayers of the exorcism ritual. It is at this point we can expect the demon to get aggressive and use Anna in other ways to prevent us from continuing."

"What other ways?"

"The demon will most likely use Anna's voice to beg us to stop. It will tell us we are hurting her and how we are only making it worse for her. You need to remember it will not be Anna speaking those words, it is simply the demon trying to manipulate us. It is this part which is the hardest for those in the room closest to the victim, for they are unable to determine the truth from the lies, and this is what the demon feeds off. You must let me lead the ritual, don't at any point engage it in conversation or believe what it says."

When dusk fell, the priest donned his surplice, and the group made their way upstairs. The atmosphere in the house felt tense with each step bringing them closer to Anna's salvation or their demise. They huddled together outside the door, listening to the raspy sounds of Anna's laboured breathing before the cold air hit them as they pushed the door open.

Anna was asleep, her face contorted in malaise. Her breath could be seen, as she exhaled, and the smell emanating from her bed was horrendous. She had soiled herself, and the room was filled with the ripe stench of decay. It was as though the bowels of Hell had opened up in the bedroom. Doctor Kashani walked over to the monitors and looked at the screen.

"I don't even know how this is possible," she said, covering her nose and mouth with one hand in an attempt to mask the smell. "I've never seen anything like this before. Her blood pressure is off the scale, she should be in cardiac arrest with vitals like these. Yet her pulse is so faint. None of it makes any sense." As she reached to take Anna's wrist in her hand, Anna's eyes opened, and she turned her head towards the doctor.

Snatching her wrist from the doctor's hand, Anna snarled as she gripped the doctor by the arm. Her fingernails dug into the skin, making the other woman cry out in pain.

"So, he's invited you to our little gathering here too, Doctor," growled a voice from deep within Anna. "You aren't his usual type. He prefers his cunt younger. Or are you fucking the other one? They both like it young," the voice jeered.

"Let me go!" cried Doctor Kashani, "I'm just trying to help Anna."

"Anna?" the voice scorned. "That bitch doesn't need any help from you. I'm the one keeping her alive now, not you."

"You are killing her," said Father Byrne sternly as he stepped forward towards the bed. "Now let her go."

"Which one?" sneered the entity as Anna's face turned towards the doctor. "Perhaps I like this one better, she is a pretty little thing, and she is feisty; I can smell it on her," Anna's hand dropped its grip on the doctor's arm and reached down to grope the doctor between the legs as the entity inside her laughed. "I like it when they put up a fight, they taste better."

Doctor Kashani staggered back, almost falling into the priest.

"Vade Retro Satana," commanded the priest, making the sign of the cross. "In the name of our Lord Jesus Christ, I command you Satan to be gone."

The entity stopped laughing to study Father Byrne with mocking intent.

"Come closer, and I'll tell you why I like this one so much," it smirked.

The priest remained in place.

"No. Why you like her is of no importance. You are not welcome, and you are implored by the power of the Lord Jesus Christ to leave this woman."

"Tell me, Father, how is your relationship with God these days? Has he forgiven you yet? You see, we aren't that different, you and me. Except the bodies I lay claim to have at least given their consent."

James and Doctor Kashani saw the priest waver for a moment as his face whitened, and he had to reach a hand out to steady himself on the nearby monitor.

"I command you, unclean spirit, along with all your minions now attacking this servant of God, by the mysteries of the incarnation, passion, resurrection, and ascension of our Lord Jesus Christ, by the descent of the Holy Spirit – "

"Touch a nerve there, did I priest?" sneered the entity. "Not the only thing being touched. Do they know what you have done?" it raised a hand to gesture towards the other two in the room.

The priest continued, gripping his chest as he shouted at the demon. "By the coming of our Lord for judgement, that you tell me by some sign your name, and the day and hour of your departure. I command you, moreover to obey me to the letter, I who am a minister of God despite my unworthiness –"

"Unworthiness," it howled. "Child fucker. Cunt! He got one pregnant, would you believe? What happened to her, priest? Oh yes, you killed her and the wretched spawn growing in her belly. Couldn't have that getting out now, could you?"

Father Byrne's face had turned ashen. He looked as though he could pass out.

"They found her at the bottom of the lake. Bloated and swollen, she didn't look so pretty after all those weeks in the water, did she? Pity, as she had so much potential. I might have tried my hand at her myself had you not got there first," it mocked.

James stepped forward to speak, unable to hold his tongue any longer.

"Release my wife now!"

Anna's head turned to James, and her face broke out into a twisted, scornful smile.

"It speaks. Since we are on the subject of confessions, do you have any of your own to make, James? We can all get to know each other a little better. I hear Soho is a nice place to visit, this time of an evening. It's been a little while for you, hasn't it? By your standards, anyway. This is turning into quite the party; it seems we've all got rather a lot in common. Preying on the weak and vulnerable. Tell me, which of us is really the worst?"

James moved forward and grabbed Anna's body by the throat.

"You cunt!" he roared.

Anna's face turned blue, yet the sneer remained in place as both the doctor and priest wrestled with him to release her.

"You aren't helping her, James!" Doctor Kashani pleaded. "Remember your wife is in there, but this is not her speaking!"

James relaxed his grip and took a step back, covering his face with his hands in desperation at the situation. "This isn't working," he wailed.

Father Byrne took his place again at the side of the bed with renewed vigour, having tossed the book aside.

"None of us are anything like you. We have all done things we are ashamed of, some of us more than others, but we are united in our determination to expel you from this woman. We will cast you out, unclean spirit, and send you back to the depths of Hell where you belong. You are not welcome in this world, and you are no longer to be a part of it."

Father Byrne drew from his pocket a vial filled with holy water.

"What's that? Keep that away from me," it hissed.

The priest opened the vial and threw the contents over Anna.

Her body writhed in pain. Her skin puckered and blistered in response as it came into contact with the water.

"It burns!" screamed the entity.

"There is more where that came from," barked the priest as he reached within his robes.

"No more! No more!" it pleaded, but this time the voice was that of a young girl. "Please, Father."

The whiteness had returned to the priest's face as he faltered at the sound of the voice.

"No, it can't be," he whispered.

"Why did you have to hurt me? I did everything you asked," begged the soft Irish voice from deep within Anna.

"No, no. I'm sorry…I never meant –"

Father Byrne staggered backwards, his hand on his chest as if he were having a heart attack. He fell backwards into a chair and clutched his chest, gasping.

"Father!" yelled James. "Remember what you told us, he will use our weakness to make us turn on each other. Don't let him win!"

The priest was inconsolable and seemed deaf to James' words. Years of pent-up guilt, shame, and anguish poured from the old man as he rocked back and forth, wailing.

"I'm sorry, I'm sorry!" he groaned in anguish.

James turned back to look at Anna. The monitors were beeping, and Doctor Kashani was frantically reattaching the wires Anna had ripped from her body when she was struck with the holy water. As he walked over to the bed, he saw for the first time, since she had been hospitalised, that she looked like herself again.

"Help me, James. Please." Anna's voice spoke to him softly as she lifted a hand to him. In a moment of lucidity, he saw the pain in her eyes, and they were her gentle, blue eyes again, not those of the entity who had looked at him so scornfully. "It's time to let me go," she whispered as the tears fell from her eyes. "You must do it now, while it's still me."

James glanced at the doctor, who had paused at the sound of Anna's voice and turned to look at them.

"Doctor, would you give us a minute?"

Doctor Kashani looked hesitant and glanced over at the priest who was beside himself, lost in a world of shame from decades ago. "James, I'm really not sure about this.

The priest told us of what might happen if we couldn't keep her alive."

"Please. It's time. Don't you think she has been through enough? Plus, this only attached itself to Anna because she invited it, so it can't harm us. The best thing we can do for Anna is to let her go peacefully."

Doctor Kashani nodded reluctantly in agreement and turned to leave the room.

Inside, Anna was screaming at James not to let her die. The entity knew she had no strength left to fight and, having drained her physically, it needed a new host. It had used her voice to persuade James into thinking she was asking him to help her die. She knew now it was too late to be saved. What would happen next, she did not know, but the time had come, and she was too weak to stop it. As the pillow came down to rest over her face, she fought from within her paralysed body, but to no avail. Darkness swept over her, and she could feel herself falling into the abyss as the sound of her husband weeping began to be drowned out by the cacophony of wails from the depths of Hell below.

23

The next few months went by in a blur for James. He had to declare Anna's death the following day and, shortly afterwards, he heard Doctor Kashani had resigned from the medical profession. Several weeks later, he read in the local paper that Father Byrne had hung himself. He had left a suicide note confessing to the murder of a young girl he had impregnated before joining the priesthood and the subsequent murder of the girl from Grožnjan. He could no longer live with the guilt, nor did he feel he deserved to live. His priest robes had been folded up neatly beside him, with the accompanying note, before he took to the noose.

Anna's funeral had been a quiet affair, mostly down to James having isolated his wife from her friends and family, so she had very little left in the way of people left who cared for her.

He had considered selling the house, but since Anna's death, he had developed a strange sense of attachment towards it. In some ways, it made him feel closer to her. The activity had ceased, and, for a time, James had felt at peace. He tried to make amends with his past, cutting down on the drinking, curbing his sex addiction, and making an effort at work to be more tolerable. His colleagues had rallied round him after the death of Anna, and he was touched by their support.

One evening, he decided to join his team for drinks after work. There was a new lady who had started in his team some weeks back who had caught his eye. It had been some time since Anna's death, and the loneliness had started to creep in.

Julia reminded him of Anna in many ways. Not just in looks, for she too was a blue-eyed redhead, but her infectious smile and flirtatious manner stirred feelings deep within him. She was new to the area, as well as the company, and didn't say much about where she had come from, but James didn't care. A couple of his colleagues had teased him that he had met his match with Julia, and she intrigued him considerably.

They hit it off well over drinks, and James decided it was time he let himself move on after Anna. It had been almost a year, and the visions of her which had plagued his dreams had, for the most part, subsided.

James invited Julia back to the house that night, and as they stumbled through the door in their drunken state, neither of them noticed the figure concealed in the shadows, watching them from the darkened living room as they headed upstairs, clutching a bottle of wine.

It was only the following morning, when Julia woke and complained of being disturbed by scratching noises that sounded like they were coming from within the walls, that James felt his world come crashing down around him. Julia's words rang in his ears as the fear which had accompanied him during Anna's demise crept up on him once more. The nightmare he thought had ended was resuming all over again as he came to the realisation Anna had been a mere conduit in pursuit of his destruction, leaving him to be perpetually plagued with this torment for the rest of his days.

EPILOGUE

Belial smiled, watching from the shadows. This one had been too easy. He liked James, so he wouldn't drive him out just yet. Not while this despicable human could feed him with what he needed. For James preyed on the weak and the vulnerable, much like himself. It made for a lucrative partnership. The demon had used many over the years, as he had resided within the confines of this house, but none had been as enjoyable as this.

He would drive James mad in time, and he would end up in the same wretched establishment as his wife, but not before he had his fill. There was far too much fun to be had first. While James still had his youth and good looks, he would be of fine use. He toyed with the idea of inhabiting James; his thirst for sex was so great he knew it would be easy, and Belial could of course take any form he wanted. He knew what James liked and what earthly pleasures he could enjoy with him as his host.

But oh, how he had feasted on Anna. She had been every bit as exquisite as he had imagined. As much as he had enjoyed feeding off their fear, the lust and vengeance tasted even better, and she had provided so much of that. Her husband had, of course, made it so easy to fuel the fire within his wife; she had just needed a little encouragement.

The voice in her head, the devil on her shoulder, the beast inside.

About The Author

Maria Kovac is an award nominated author, known most for her published works on Medium and as dark fiction editor for Agency Magazine. *The Devil's Claim* is her debut novella. She has a penchant for dark, transgressive fiction, folk horror and paranormal romance. Her short story, *The Cursed,* is available to purchase in paperback and on Kindle. Her Nordic folk horror *Lullaby,* is due for release in 2026.
Follow Maria on;
Medium: medium.com/@maria.kovac
Twitter: x.com/mkovac_writer
Instagram: @author_mkovac

Afterword

My thanks, first and foremost, goes to my editor, Stephen Black for making this happen. The concept behind *The Devil's Claim* was one I had carried for years but a conversation with Stephen turned this idea into the book you are reading today. I have always been fascinated by cases of demonic possession but most of what I had seen and read had been from the perspective of those on the outside looking in and I wanted to create something which tapped into the mind of the person possessed and that is how Anna was created.

An extended thanks also goes to the wider Black Thoughts Editorial team for their input and support. I also wish to thank Christy Aldridge at Grim Poppy Design for the cover artwork.

Lastly, a big thank you to my friends and family who have supported me on this journey.

Also By The Author

The Cursed

Tröjsto, a small mining community on the Swedish-Finnish border, is a town cursed. Plagued by the undead who surface from the abandoned mines to descend upon the town each winter as darkness sets in. No longer able to protect themselves and shunned by their southern neighbours, a small team decides to take matters into their own hands. They will do anything to protect their own even if that means having to sacrifice others.

Printed in Dunstable, United Kingdom